Brief Cases
Short Spans

Also by Tom Sheehan

NOVELS:
An Accountable Death
Vigilantes East
Death for the Phantom Receiver

POETRY:
Ah, Devon Unbowed
The Saugus Book
Reflections from Vinegar Hill
This Rare Earth & Other Flights
The Westering

MEMOIR
A Collection of Friends

SHORT STORY COLLECTION
Epic Cures

NONFICTION:
A Gathering of Memories, Saugus 1900-2000
(with John Burns)
Of Time and the River, Saugus 1900-2006
(with John Burns and Robert Wentworth)

BRIEF CASES
SHORT SPANS

Short Stories By

TOM SHEEHAN

Press 53
Winston-Salem, NC

Press 53
PO Box 30314
Winston-Salem, NC 27130

First Edition

Cover design by Kevin Watson
Cover Photo, "Burnside Bridge," by Jeff Fioravanti

Printed on acid-free paper
ISBN: 978-0-9816280-5-9

Dedication

For Saugus's John Burns,
Bob Wentworth,
Neil Howland,
The ROMEOs (Retired Old Men Eating Out),
Extraordinary readers, gabbers,
and dear companions.

And for our town
which gave so much to us
and for which we tried to make
our small payback
with
The Saugus books,
A Gathering of Memories
and *Of Time and the River*.

Some will know the joy we shared
and the others can find out.

Acknowlegments

The author wishes to thank the editors of the following publications in which these stories first appeared, in the version presented here or an earlier version.

West47, (Galway), *Atlantic 3711* and *Ken *Again*, "Leaving for Viviers"
The Sidewalk's End, "Hand upon the Brow"
Triplopia, "The Puzzle Solution's Swift Shift from Irony"
Facets Magazine, "Salvatore Giambaressi, Numbers Runner, Reader"
Tryst, "Shag DeBrillen, Brickie"
Kudzu Monthly, Canopic Jar, "Improper Burial at the First Iron Works of
    America" and "The Cochran Resolve"
Prose Toad, "The Gang from the Boatyard"
Loch Raven Review, "The Man with Inner Movies"
Muscadine Lines, "Silent Retrieval"
Slow Trains, "Almost Rickshaw"
Ken *Again, Muscadine Lines, "Swan River Daisy"
New Works Review, "The Man Who Hid Music"
Perigee, "Apple, for Whom I Scoured the Universe"
Halfway Down the Stairs, "Home from the Dead"

Work here has merited Pushcart Prize, Million Writer, and Noted Story nominations, and has earned a Silver Rose Award and a Georges Simenon Award for short story excellence.

Contents

The Storekeeper   11

Hand Upon the Brow   24

Improper Burial at the First Iron Works of America   33

The Puzzle Solution's Swift Shift from Irony   51

Silent Retrieval   56

Salvatore Giambaressi: Numbers Runner, Reader   67

Shag Debrillen, Brickie   79

The Gang from the Boatyard   92

Man with Inner Movies   105

Home from the Dead   124

Apple, for Whom I Have Scoured the Universe   136

Strangers to Love   141

Swan River Daisy   153

The Cochran Resolve   160

Almost Rickshaw   181

The Man Who Hid Music   194

Leaving for Viviers   198

The Storekeeper

B efore I knew what was going on, at twelve years of age, I saw what was going on with Putney Grimes, who owned the Pioneer Grocery and General Store near my house, and one of his customers, Maxine Greenery. Truth of the matter was I didn't know what I was actually seeing, or couldn't understand it until much later, but parts of this life were moving around me, memories as well as history being made, records being kept, innocence being expelled one way or another, true innocence. World War II, of course, was trampling on a whole tide of innocence. Glad tidings said General MacArthur was back in the Philippines, but on the other side of that, Glenn Miller was reportedly lost in the North Sea. My mother looked dreamy-eyed at that news, the way she could share some things without talking about them. In my own little way, then with just those dozen years in hand, I knew I was part of it all, part and parcel. Pieces of it enveloped me, or lifted me, or brought me down, experience building its everlasting testimony.

As for Putney and Maxine, a warmth was in our midst, in spite of the shape of the world, even if I could not give it a name. I couldn't name it and I couldn't touch it, but it was there. It all centered in the store, small heart of the universe we knew. Much later I could call myself, in retrospect, the love child because I saw the love blooming between them right there in front of me, day by day, even though it took more than a few years time, and I, of course, in my own growth, felt the changes.

The way it was for a while was that Maxine Greenery could be a widow for all we knew, and with two sprouting boys. The hard words came one evening just as supper hit the table and twilight was still holding sway, the shadows soft, day dwindling down to its knees: her husband Harry had been declared missing, lost at sea from a destroyer in the Mediterranean Sea, half a world away, a lifetime away. Shadows joined with shadows, loss atop loss. George Drew, the fire chief, brought the word. He was the self-appointed dispenser of the awful tasks in his snappy uniform, black gloves, white hat, pants pressed so that the creases were like sheet metal lines, and all blue, the length of him all blue. When he tucked his white hat under his blue arm, every person on the street knew it was not an inspection of the premises being approached, the slow walk into a front yard, the unhurried climb to the porch, the soft tap on the door. And nothing followed that first announcement of the loss of Harry. No whispers. No rumors. Loss settled on us, heavy as one could imagine.

Harry was one of the good guys around our corner before he left, and Maxine was seen as a regular customer of Putney's. She had been a customer since Harry put her in that converted barn he had worked on for Ladd Griffin just around the turn from Putney's store, when he went off in the Navy. Harry was a magician with hammer and saw, good old Harry, and had the acute eye for resurrection, bringing old lines of structures into new lines, new plumbs, walls standing the way they were meant to stand, with the good shoulders. In due time, the way promise evolves, as all the neighbors had said almost at once when he went away, that Harry would build his own house when he came back, when his turn came up, but those chances were now gone and slim at best, it appeared.

But the main guy here from my angle, Putney Grimes, owned and was the sole employee of the Pioneer Store in my end of town, near the first Iron Works of America that lay untouched for more than three hundred years. When my pals and I had a few spare coins, Putney's store was where we ended up, a post-

Depression magnet for kids used to grasping. Many of my friends had found labor to our liking, our stretch to manhood, the war moving at far edges, almost visible, the way we saw the Newsreels at the State Theater on Saturday matinees. And we had small jobs then, paying small change. We had a lot to do with scrap metal drives, paper collections, keeping our lips zipped, pretenses of one sort or another.

Earlier, in a stretch toward manhood, we had carried baskets of manure and sterilized loam into the old mushroom house on Lily Pond. It used to be an icehouse before Freddie Rippon converted it to a mushroom house where, if the crop was fairly large and there was no disease, he could make some good money. As kids we shared that whole enterprise, eventually loading trucks going off to the market in Boston, filling our pockets with slim coins while mothers sat at their kitchen tables waiting for donations.

As it was, most of my pals had a handle on such tasks in Saugus, closing in on the mid-century mark, money times better than they had been for a handful of years, and some of the old guys that made it back from Europe and the Pacific were comfortably on leave or medically discharged, enriching all of us with new gestures, new stories, seemed like a whole new language. They brought their pieces of the world back with them, dumping much of it in our laps, the laps of those who had stayed at home, the kid brothers and kid neighbors and those who couldn't make the fit. My brother came back from the wild Pacific, right off an aircraft carrier twice hit by Kamikazes and once by a torpedo, never telling us until he got home, and my cousin Warren came back from Europe after Patton shook his hand in front of a gathering of troops out there on the edge of the Old World. Pretty special for a Saugus kid.

On the other hand, a few of their comrades managed to slip off the trains in Saugus Center near midnight, coming right out of North Station and the Army Base or the Charlestown Navy Yard, like they were total strangers. And I guess some of them were, they had changed so much, had seen so much. All their stories, though, came as gifts, long into our new nights of discovery, a new expression, a new outlook, a new hope even as we realized many of the dark parts were being glossed over. Some did not make the return trip and there was a time when I knew all their names and all their faces, what they had left in the till for me, a kid from this end of town.

Putney's Pioneer Store was where much of the talk and information passed from hither and yon to all the houses in our end of Saugus. He carried a whole arsenal of goods besides the usual grocery items, most of the time catering to the ladies with cloth goods, small hats, big bowls; you name it and he'd get it. He specialized in information too. You could tell that Put was eager for all kinds of intelligence, as though he had been selected to be a communication center, keeping people informed, ranking news, passing tidbits that ordinarily didn't plan much hurt for anybody. Some things, I knew, he kept to himself, letting others pass the word, as if he was a sieve screening out the bad parts.

I think it was the melancholy of the war that mostly triggered Putney, changed his expression, changed his manners, and damn near changed his language. The war and its odd pieces daily came down the street and through his door like the wind had kicked it open, like the words of another telegram hitting straight at a heart or two, or a distant shot or shell seeming to come home to the storekeeper in a gulp of morning air, as though aimed at him from the very beginning. All this culminated for him in Maxine and her current status as "widow." He was the onlooker who cared even though it was at a polite distance. They regarded each other in these times with awareness, each of them at some point of loss, at loneliness or linen.

Then, in days of recovery, when the war was finally being won, Putney and Maxine were allowed to be drawn by their needs. As it stood, the future loomed lonely for both of them. When Maxine was in the store, she was always visible to Putney, who would put himself to that advantage no matter what aisle he was working in or who he was waiting on. He did it casually, not at all obvious to most other customers, but a perfect chameleon to my eyes. On odd occasions he'd let me sit beside the side door and read comic books for free, as long as I did not crease them too much. It was a measure of his charity, of the blossoms that ripened in his heart. From my spot at the side door I had a view down the front counter and down the back aisle. The first time Maxine stretched to put something back on a higher shelf, a packet or container she had dislodged from its place, I caught a half smile on Putney's face, though at the moment he was waiting on the neighborhood witch, Ethel Nourseling, my old teacher with the strap or the harsh ruler for a wayward tongue. Maxine always wore dresses that seemed to have been slipped onto her slim frame, silky and soft and smooth the way they flowed with her curves and graces and all the goodly package; that package contained blond hair soft as a summer cone, wide eyes that surprise found a good home in, lips a favored pink blossom had touched just about every time out, and a warmth, a warmth that was never spectacular, not for those of us who looked closely, but always countable, easily marked and noted, as though a small party had started someplace and she was invited.

Putney, a bachelor all the way to forty, was not a handsome dog, as one wag said, but he was neat. You might know it, grocers tend to be neat, sort of going along with the territory, everything in its place to catch they eye, the silent art of advertisement, the handless reach. Things that look good might taste good, or feel good. To boot, certain facets of Put's behavior ought to be mentioned for the best picture of him. For absolute sure, he knew the store the way a woman knows her kitchen, shelf and larder, cabinet and cupboard, the bins and barrels at the end of the main aisle like greengrocer totems, what's stacked where, or put behind, what's left in easy reach and another tucked away under the counter for special days, or consigned for the next special sale or holiday. His clock, or his calendar, was pretty near perfect for his customers, for our neighborhood. Now and then we'd see it working, the close lookers among us, like him spotting old Della Crandall coming down the street and dipping below the counter to lay out what had been hidden for more than a week, a new bolt of cloth or an infernally new utensil the adventurous lady would grab in a minute. They'd been ordered for her and salted away for the most appropriate visit, as if old Put had a hand directly on her pulse, on her current interests.

In addition, he always wore an apron that was adorned with the day's work, wore it like a good soldier wears his chevron, as one might say. He was proud of his work, his store, and he was potentially if not actually prosperous. As a stock boy he had worked there for the previous owner, went away for ten years, came back and bought the place, as if he had planned it right from the very start. His hello each morning was broad, meaningful, countable, him having risen early to greet the day, to be there before the baker and the milkman and the newsboy. Early energy became him, the quick movements, the lack of indecision, jump starts on a new day. One-man operations have to be fed that way.

His razor thin mustache was little more than a hairline's width, and moved each time he spoke, smiled or expressed want or dislike. I never really knew what color his eyes were; I guess I never really looked, though they did come off as some kind of greenish bit, sort of changeable under other expressions or enlightenment. Narrow in the waist from a lifetime of shelf stocking and lifting, and a sane and steady diet one could imagine, he moved about athletically, as if he were in a game. Neat and athletic, our grocer. On top of the small ladder he could stock the top shelves with good speed, never losing balance, reaching just far enough when he had to. The neatness advanced in order to the store's ambience, the certainty of odors that abounded on certain days, on every day of some sort or other. There came coffee grinding and candy smothering my mouth and nose the minute I entered the door. It had been that way for a couple of years, the grateful larder of the corner store, pungent and ripe and so full of goodness I could feel the blossoms of it coming into the branches of me. There was the fresh vitality of new bread, fresh baked and threatening the back of my throat, saying I could grab some and run, or scrounge for a half loaf, and worry about the butter later on. And jumped up the freshness of lettuce and husky tomatoes and apple stuff so rich it could make your knees bend. Lastly, just as threatening, came the special meat days, when pork came on the run or cow's liver or lamb kidneys advanced a whole new odor the kitchen got ripe with. Some days it could have been the edge of the slaughterhouse dumped on us, or the block outside Kmita's chicken house where the ax swung in morning sunlight and I could see a hen's last roost as darkness came close to it. I finally figured a whole lot of it out, all on my own. I had always been hungry, the Depression Kid always with an angle toward food.

Once, just as the door opened and a whistle of wind came about, or an airy breath because it was spring, Putney came to attention. I caught the scent too, the fragrance, not of the day or the May smells that came along in with it, like new leaves and new blooms and the old earth winding itself up again, but another and newer one, especially for me… and old Put, hardly paying attention the minute before, spun on his heels and Maxine was there, slim as ever, in her light blue dress sitting on her like a blossom, inhabiting the doorway. There was first the alert of fragrance, then the heart of fragrance, and a rocking in our souls, in deeply where it must count, where redolence, known, gathers all kinds of reactions. It was a sharing, that frequency coming on air, a quite special broadcast of a special bouquet. It fully carried Maxine on those private sheets of air.

And old Putney was at heads up. And Maxine glowed her usual warmth, as if she belonged in that place more than any place else, in the midst of all the sensual goodness. To my eye he and Maxine each had a fair amount of grace. I think, even from my angle, I put them together before they were together, though I'd never be sure of the timing.

Some of it meant, at least for me, that it was okay for them to look upon each other, that it was okay to look good, look neat, look to one's best advantage, if merely for the looking. It was permission from two lonely people not saying a word about such acceptance. Every time a teacher said, "Neatness counts," I was alert to Putney and Maxine, if but the extension of their images working the back of my head like a piece of a black and white film. Now and then, of course, in my mind's eye, going through my own exploding new dimensions, I was alert to her preparations, as to how she primped and primed herself, where she sent the kids while she did so, at least not alerting them that their mother was being a bit selfish, reaching out in a most harmless way but behind a closed door, locked away with herself and whoever might be tempting her company.

Putney was harmless from any standpoint, but he had keen eyes. I was always sure that she knew about his eyes. And I knew how her dress slipped easily onto her frame, thought of how she might have shrugged but a single shoulder to let it fall gracefully in place, and fully assumed that Putney had the same picture, the soft sounds of elegance and mystery coming together in the same motion, the same slow blur of beauty that might be slipping into place from a simple shrug.

When Doug Matlick's body was shipped home from a Marine plane crash in North Carolina and lowered into the Veteran's Section of our cemetery, I was there with my father who had been in the Marines. It was his own salute to Doug. Doug was Harry's best friend. Putney saluted too, the only time I ever saw him in a suit, plain and gray and new looking, and never once looking at Maxine the way he did in the store, for Maxine was there, being an old friend of Doug's. Before I knew it, we were there again, for another of Harry's friends who had come home for good, almost able to touch his old pal and teammate Doug, for they were now part of a new huddle in a corner of the cemetery, close as they ever were. For sure, teammates again.

I knew every face at both services and the burials and could mark each of them in their places around town, and felt all the sadness you could expect a body to hold. I didn't cry, though, did not a shed tear, but when I looked at Putney I saw he was shaken past his roots. It was as if everything all the others had felt closed in around him, and around Maxine who only once turned and looked at him with the most serious look I had seen in a long time. It was as if she had spoken, but with silence.

I watched them for two years as the slim war victories became big victories, and more of them came rousing across the face of the globe. The two of them eventually seemed to grow toward each other without really knowing how close they were.

Wiley Okens said at The Vets one night that "them two ought to find how to scratch each other's backs 'stead of sparrin' around like pretending." Many folks in town knew that Maxine was finding a bit of release in Putney from what was hounding her, the squeezed pillow, the silent nights. Putney allowed her more than a sense of hope, but all of it at a distance no matter how close they got on days she came to the store to pick up a few things for the house. Even when there were days it came off as mere exercise to walk to the store and go away empty-handed, she did not leave with an empty heart. Yet, at forty years of age, distilled in his manners and outlook, damn near cemented in place if not character, Putney had that one old-time speed. Of course, Maxine's two boys would now and then enter into the slow-moving stand-off of sorts, tipping the scales in pro and con arguments the way kids do more than people realize. Malcolm Burdus the undertaker offered, "One mouth advanced to four mouths is some kind of algebra no matter what math says."

Putney's down to earth and thoughtful approach was appreciated by those who voiced opinions on romance, illicit or otherwise. "He don't rush that girl out of her boots none at all," Malcolm told Wiley one night and later on said, "If he don't hurry up, I'm going to beat him to it." All of them somehow knew that Putney had ceased a regular Saturday night removal from town that was seen as a concession to Maxine and the space that had grown in his heart.

"Hell," Wiley replied, "he's got all the time in the world, Malcolm, and you got all the room in the earth. But I'm suspecting that ole Put has just that one speed and we ain't seen it yet." So the talk moved on about them, and the store leaped upon good days for Putney when Maxine came in through that front door like spring was sliding around behind her playing games.

All the time, no matter how we read it, the unknown sat on the face of each of them, the uncertainty, the Fates that move all around us like the tides on a beach, touching, drawing back, nipping and tapping, neap and run, like the manner of unvoiced threats and promises.

As it turned out, things happened at night to old Putney. It was always at night or the approach of night as it gathered down the street or from across town and he could feel a descent coming down around him.

One evening, almost to closing time on one of his late night closings, a shower and a visit to the library ahead of him, two young fellows robbed bachelor Putney of what was in the till. The eleven dollars, all singles, were hardly worth their efforts, as he had hidden under darkness the balance of the day's take inside a pair of rubber boots hanging on the wall behind the counter, safe enough for the bank in the morning. But one of the young fellows snatched a candy bar as he and his companion were leaving with their eleven-dollar gain. It was a Sky Bar. All Putney could think of was somehow getting a box of candy to Maxine, then he realized he hadn't been shot for eleven dollars. He told that to the police chief, in so many words.

Then, on another night in our local history, without notice or fanfare, from what unknown terrors he had been caught up in, and much older, Harry came home, came into the store late, as if riding the darkness itself, the ghost of all ghosts, despite the edge of his voice yet still haggard and not at all like his old self. He hailed Putney from the door. "Hey, Put," he said, "howdy partner, I'm going up to surprise Maxine. Got a nice box of candy for me? Good as you got. I ain't got much else to carry."

Putney would never forget those words of Harry's.

If it was a bad turn and a bad year for Putney, it was a bad year for Harry too. And also for Maxine, as one could imagine. Harry, after the quick celebration and a hundred stories taking all kinds of shapes, the dark and the doomed, filled with odd characters and fairy people, ogres and demons of all measures and reaches, drank from one end of the day to the other. For a whole year he didn't pick up a hammer or a saw. Maxine once in a while would come into the store with a puffy lip, or a tear in her eye. Put had to look away, mind his own business, fall out of love if he could, for beyond all things that mattered it was a hopeless situation. She was hurting and Put stopped looking at her the way he had for those few years of his dependence on her.

The story that made the rounds was indeed bizarre, if anything more bizarre than war can be, and rescue at the ends of desperation. Harry, it was learned, was pulled from the Mediterranean by a French fisherman and hidden in the fisherman's house. For a long while he was tucked away in a secret space in the attic of the fisherman's house, where, through one small opening above an eave he could watch the small village square as it revolved under the war and under Nazi occupation. One hellacious day he saw the Germans execute three American fliers right in the square and saw their bodies dropped into a hole, doused with gasoline, and torched. When the fire died out, the remains were covered over at the end of the day, interred right in the square of the little village. Three days later, when house searches were renewed by the Germans, the fisherman moved Harry to another house and a secret room whose access was halfway down the depth of an old well in the cellar. That "hole in the wall" led to a spacious room dug into the hillside many years earlier for a different cause. The new "landlord" had a daughter, Yvette, just 17, who shined on Harry and visited him at least once a week and often stayed most of the night. When she became pregnant, it was apparent the family wanted to keep Harry under cover for as long as they could. Yvette gave birth to a son, and Harry was kept in the room some months after the war was over before he climbed out one night and made his escape.

He fled his European life.

But, as one must realize, the memories of Yvette, and the memory of another son, never quite left Harry. Maxine never admitted to knowing, but she must have known some of the mystery. Harry's long incarceration, the visitations of his young lover, the subsequent son, all hounded him no end. All of it had followed him home to Maxine and the two boys and the subsequent nightly visits, away from home, to bar after frivolous bar, to friend after frivolous friend. The pattern was constant and unbreakable and the deadly inroads were open.

We did not hear the stories come up as spoken history here in town; they drifted in on their own feet, on an everywhichway wind from odd sources coming across town lines by postmen, taxi drivers, delivery men, the coal man Merv Takens who thought Harry should be hospitalized because he had flown on that same flight of alcohol. Problems knocking at Harry's heels were openly discussed in the barber shop, the post office, and in our own bars, though never in the ear of Harry on his way back to the house after a night on the next town, or the one beyond that. After a while we could picture him being followed, ghostlike, by his French lover and mother of his son, and the son himself. That had to be a bear to carry on one's back already borne to drop weights easier than promises.

One night, the moon behind a sudden cloud, mist rising as from the earth the way fog walks on water and roadways and intemperate reaches, history making new demands, life itself asking for settlements, Harry was killed as he walked across the turnpike from one bar to the next, going from John's Bar to Ma Taylor's Kitchen across Route One. One of his own drinking buddies ran him down, never seeing him on the dark road, never seeing the dark specters stepping right out behind his drinking pal, never seeing those who were keeping Harry company.

Putney, to his everlasting credit, started all over. And I watched him again, from a new perspective and a new awareness, only this time he must have measured time and what had been eaten up of that which had been granted to him in the first place. For he picked up some speed in his delivery, like he was coming right out of the bullpen at Fenway Park.

One night a few months later he carried with him his best box of candy and Maxine opened the door for him. Putney the storekeeper shifted directly into second gear. Nothing was ever the same again.

Hand Upon the Brow

B riggs Wragrum's life as an expiator began early.

It was not announced or decided; no telegrams or headlines or heart murmurs propounded it. It just happened that way, a long time ago. At odd moments I can bring back a deal of his industry, as an observer from various vantages, now and then fair portions of that observation given over from a few close friends, gossip traveling the streets, from Briggs's friends as well as mine. That early beginning, though, must have caused Briggs untold moments of frustration, his keeping his own counsel from day one. Briggs's brother Shag said it outright and on many occasions, tipping his head at first in odd salute, later his drink: *my brother's no snitch.*

Shag's eyes could tear a face apart if let be. But Shag did not know it all.

And I, observer of ordinary means but devoted, had to piece most of it together from the outside. Oh, I knew both of them, Briggs and Shag, in the hallways dark as Hades, in dank-dark-dismal cold-water tenement cellars full of tricks and ruses of games deep as hide-n-seek, on starry roof-tops where we shared basketfuls of moonlight, pigeons we made out doves, dreams set out on the horizons floating away from us on city light fringes, and the ensuing darkness that unknown outlands sent back in silent stretches of night. The small band of us, mixed bag and blessing, tossed into the cauldron of shaping, came off as survivors with wide talents; we could shinny up or down downspouts from bedroom windows no matter the height, scale innumerable walls, hide when not yet dark, find a mouthful in barren pantries or ice boxes. Hungry, ever cool or hot in the grip of the Depression, we lived paired up with dreams and rock-hard fists.

And this journal of Briggs the Expiator, from the first day observing, was locked in my head as tight as one of those fists. Only an expanse of time could free it.

Or headlines.

The youngster Shag came out of the four-story tenement building's rear door onto Ferrin Street and the road-wide bulge of cobblestones, the late afternoon sun bouncing sheen on the cobblestone pan faces, the gutter an electric ribbon lit up. Behind him lay the dim interior of the cold-water flats, clutter haven, abysmal, usually rank; there, like marks of the century, hallway wallpaper hung loose in wide sheets or acres of it lost to the trash bin, paint non-existent or near so on every wooden surface, a damp nose-filling odor of bad fruit hanging in the air that assailed him in the halls, otherwise empty even of sound. The metallic ceilings of the hallways were gnarled with seas or clouds of rust. Yet the kitchen he left had a worn shine on linoleum, a small counter with scrubbed surface, a sink that seemed not to have collected a dirty dish, in a corner a prim stovetop almost at luster. These he left behind him, and he was sure a look to the end of Ferrin Street would not bring an image of his father coming home from the docks, the heavy shoulders lowered at wages, head bent in solace, three- and four-deckers burying him in shade nearly clandestine. The out-world father was forever cast in shadow, in doubt, into questions at times about his salutary being. Shag couldn't remember the last time he had seen the breadwinner in daylight, and now and then, as if spectered, he came but a voice in the night, and a voice not to be intruded on.

Shortly thereafter into one pocket, the movement as sly and quicker than could be discerned by the most watchful of store clerks, six-year-old Shag Wragrum, a smiling, disarmingly-sweet-faced tow-headed youngster, wearing a black jacket, a faint red signal like a nova star from birth decorating the higher bridge of his nose, one eye tooth apparently winning a battle against the others in his mouth, slipped a candy bar into a wide pocket of his flannel jacket. He could, that boy, lean against a wall as if he had not taken a breath in half an hour, at least not an exuberant breath. Shade or shadow he could be, or a still piece of cast light; dismantled, innominate by choice, ill defined, all at once.

The candy bar cost all of a nickel.

Less than an hour later, under the eyes of the same custodian of the small variety store in Boston's Charlestown district, and right across the street from the main gate of the Navy Yard, Shag's equally sweet-faced twin brother Briggs, his nose likewise marked with the faint red spot denoting something deeper than brotherhood, a similar tooth at odds with his others, blood pumping danger and excitement through his heart in small bursts, placed a restituted candy bar back into the same open candy box on an old door set on barrels in the store. Thirty open boxes of candy with all their toothless intentions graced the spread of that door in the store's small interior. Outside the wind announced intentions on all windows, February calling out its name down the length of the city street and against frail and opaque protection. The clerk Kosko the Pole said, "Want nothin'?" and Briggs, coming past his brother's shadow, said, "Naw, I gotta go wait supper," to which Kosko smiled his disbelief.

Briggs Wragrum's life as an expiator, seemingly, had begun that day. Years would add burden to the weight that it was, time upon time, incidents galore. Yet the toothy boy never backed off, never argued or castigated, never remonstrated. Fate had waved its wand.

From the very beginning it was set. When Briggs and Shag Wragrum were born mere minutes apart, to their mother's surprise and their father's consternation and endless doubt about his place in the world, one fortuitous star intervened for the pair, as did one black star without light for a million or more years, a star deep in an endless black void setting adrift across space a moaning sound no ear could misunderstand. Down the birth canal Briggs came warm and cuddly and ahead of the troop of two, seeking early comfort, and Shag, cut off in the underpass, his nose too bearing emblazoned red, came scratching and seeking an edge so early in life. The lines and facets of their being were cut and polished; one a giver and one a taker.

And Ilka Wragrum knew it before they were a year old. Alone seven days a week, her husband drawn forever into pier politics, a stevedore marked by cause and loud imploration and profanity, she had the glory of time and thought, idle and otherwise.

From thence the disparities of the twins did not so much collide as carom and fall into the other's track, often going in opposite directions in tangential reactions. The mother saw them off one day, to visit friends. They'd been in school half a year then. From her window, remembered to a later day, she saw them leaving, stopping at the curbing, one going left and one going right, in their own pursuits. Perhaps that day, she thought continually, the carving of souls was making its ultimate cut, shaping forever what was to come. A shrug she also remembered, perhaps a shivering aspect about her body, and a dark and cool presence invading her most private self, beyond that core where nobody could enter in passion, in either guard or disregard. Knowledge without a voice.

It was the flannel-mouthed Mrs. Lopelli from the third-floor tenement directly across Ferrin Street, sticking her nose in again, who mouthed it in her own fashion, "How come them boys don't keep company wid each other, strange, eh, Mrs. *Rugrump?*" Word selection often was one of her armaments in this new world, a cute, sometimes snide way of making points on those about her, putting them in their place she so thought. Having shaken a dust mop out the window, she was watching her neighbor's sons as well as noting the small cloud, in layers catching sunlight in narrow city travails, settling its light matter on the street. The cool air of the fateful day seemed to weigh the dust down.

Mrs. Lopelli's massive breasts flopped their milky abundance on the windowsill and Ilka Wragrum could still hear the guys on the corner talking about *The Feeder*. "There's one will never fall on her face, boys. Won't be permitted." Guffaws, elbows in the ribs, snide-induced snide smiles as secret as gossip of the streets. The hugely endowed one would offer, more in statement than question, "You'd think so close together in coming they'd be pals forever, but it don't look like it, eh, Mrs. *Rugrump*?" Her head made a little aberrant toss as if a most proper punctuation mark was being made, adjudicated: *this foreigner, this Slavvie,* at least, *marked.*

What neither woman knew, and would not know for a good number of years: Briggs Wragrum always knew where his brother was, who he was with, and often had a damned good idea of what he was up to. So elementary it had become, knowing where a peer was, what route took him there and back, what kind of people peopled those polar routes. The decisions made on those routes or because of those routes were harder to detect, but clues lay everywhere for the observant. Early on, by fate or some other selection process none of the characters were aware of, Briggs became, as a company of one, for his lone brother the self-appointed chaperon, watchdog, guardian at a distance, the brother Cerberus. In Shag's tracks he followed for much of his life, and just about all of it early on. That he would love his brother all his life was unquestioned, but he loved his mother more. Her love, visible as a flag, never wavered. He'd never let it be at half mast. Not in this lifetime. Not this boy.

"Oh, Briggsy," she had said once in a fleet of secrecy, "he's a bit more daring than you, but has less judgment. Watch always for me. Always." To her own ample bosom she had drawn her son, her loving, most trusted hand brushing full confidence across his head in a salute the years would remember, no other hand ever again touching him with such grace, or with such command.

All for him was sworn.

The single dollar bill slipped out of a visiting Aunt Grace's pocketbook, Shag dropping a newspaper over the open handbag and slipping his fingers into green depth, bought a supply of candy;

but before the visit was over, from inside his own secret repository, Briggs Wragrum replaced the dollar bill with one he had earned from his small paper route. "You have such darling boys, Ilka," the aunt said, smothering both of them with loud, wet kisses. "God, I could steal off with them if they was but a little older." The currency exchange, never noted by anyone other than the watchdog brother, was just another parentally undetected sin of the star-shadowed brother.

There was a mix of coins taken from a desk at school when they were in the sixth grade at the Kent School. Briggs was found coming out a cellar window well after midnight. The principal, at first questioning the contents of the milk money jar, said there was not a penny missing, but that the coinage assembled seemed different. Briggs was scolded but said he had been trying to prove someone could get into the school after dark. He said he worried about it. Shag never said a word to anybody, content to be himself, to let stand what he had wrought after dark.

Ilka Wragrum hugged her warmest son.

Their young lives, into early teens, were spent in a mad flux, and in hasty retreats where decision and command were presences. At stickball on the quiet column of Ferrin Street, they were connoisseurs, broom handles wielded like saber whips, driving the half-balls two to three light poles worth, driving runners ahead of them, sending roars up the shaky sides of tenement buildings that took them and hid them at night. At this they excelled, the pair of them, earning fabulous and infamous nicknames eventually finding their way onto wide doors, walls, cellar beams, hallways in the dim stairwells to the upper reaches of three and four floor tenements, their earliest escape from *igcogniti* to *graffiti*. *The Golddust Twins* was carved, painted or crayoned, and *Two-for-four-or-more*, or the *Pair of Hits*, or *We Are the Ones*!

Ilka Wragrum, graffiti scanning, would know a dark secret, seeing one son a scribe, one not. Without doubt those free moments of her young athletes, under her gaze from the high window, were the best of times; they were observed, they were safe, they had no secrets worth any diversion at game time. It was, other than small providence, the opportunity for the small pain in her upper chest to fade away as if it had never been there in the first place. Perhaps, she might think, one day's pain does not carry over to the next. Strange ideas cure strange ailments she assured herself. Even with flannel-mouth across the way sharing her small joy, she counted those moments as the lucky ones, for herself, for her children dashing in the street below.

For the boys there were game chases across the tops of near-connected tenements, leaps involved, daring and agility coming as near to apoplexy as an adult watcher could maximize and tolerate. Athletes they were, the pair of them, and each with their own secret, for Shag went his own way at thievery with like minions and Briggs, his mother's hand forever across his brow, followed in expiation.

Probably the one daunting moment in all of this for Briggs was the Whiting's milk wagon episode, a quick deviation from his normal behavior, and yet one of those stop-and-gos that come along in life: forever after he remembered the abrasive Rorschach of rust left scored on his right leg, from knee to ankle and all down the calf muscle, when it was caught for fearful seconds in the wheel spokes of the milk wagon he had hopped on, grabbing the tailgate with two sure hands and throwing his feet in on top of the axle.

Six years old at the time, his life could have been seriously changed in another second. It was studiously apparent. The absolute clock of clocks he knew then, saw the second hand move hesitatingly and incredulously slow, heard the private ticking as dim as a pocket watch tucked away at the end of a fob, found all about him a salient and clear-cut sense of measurement. Never would he forget, never had he forgotten that moment, the near-vise grip of it with all attendance, horse's hooves clopping their deliberateness on the cobblestones, the ignorant milkman in the driver's seat whistling an old song, air filled with the smell of the horse, sour milk, manure hanging in place; his leg being squeezed

by spoke rotation, panic smell beginning to rise in his nose as
thick as burnt rubber or new road tar, and the glorious Saturday
morning sun on his back when he was freed of that rude clasping.

"Shag," he said, limping but safe aboard the sidewalk, rubbing
his leg that in another second might have been wrenched from
him, torn asunder from the hip, or bent and misshapen forever,
Shag knowing the small miracle, "I know I was saved." They
vowed never to hop milk wagons ever again, so help me God,
each one taking from the escape a sense of value, neither one
knowing their mother, hands clasped, a minor sense of horror
having passed through her as sure as the evil torment promising
explosion in her body, watched from her window. And torn by the
promises of her sons as much as that which had invaded her body.
She could not put names to any of the intrusions.

Whenever Briggs wanted that moment and all that gave it
company, a new day being spoiled by his brother, new release on
the horizon, it was there for him. It shaped much of his life, as
much a tool of his shaping as his brother's ways, or his mother's
imploration with her hand of faith across his brow. That other
message she had sent he had not fathomed as yet, or dared not. It
was as if there was something else unsaid but to be understood.
He dared not ask her what that message was. He would not ask
Shag.

At the wharf one night their father disappeared, too noisy at
work, too much mouth for some and spokesman for others. He
went off as if he really was an invisible man in their lives. The only
trace could be the ponderous Atlantic, repository of innumerable
sins, crowd cover of the widest order. The boys cried, Ilka
Wragrum knew again the silent pain coursing freely through body.
Debating within herself their lives coming she saw Briggs in
command, Shag following, and knew it to be mere argument for
the sake of argument. Pain, she knew, had other names.

The boys were seventeen when her soul was finally eaten up
by her body and their aunt provided a roof for them, a room at the
end of the hall on another third floor, one block closer to City

Square, one block up-town. When Shag stole a car and left it at the corner, practically under the window of that room, Briggs snuck out after midnight and drove it to the school grounds and left it there. Hand upon the brow.

A week later there was a robbery at Abie's Market a few blocks away. The next night, well after midnight, another window was broken at Abie's. The fat little storekeeper found his stolen money on the floor beneath the broken window. All Charlestown knew that Shag had scored and Briggs had replied. Hand upon the brow.

The coverage continued for a number of years, and the split widened, transgressor and expiator at their chosen rounds. But there never was a blow-up, never a confrontation between the brothers that any of us knew of, never a finger pointed. Old timers shook their heads, never having seen the likes of the pair. Hand upon the brow.

When a sixteen-year-old neighbor, Camp Judey, became pregnant, local denizens figured the stonewall had been met; Briggs tried again, but not so eagerly. Finally a difference had risen. Hand upon the brow.

Of course I have to report it ended when the whole world dumped down on that other hand, in the other hand, in Shag's hand. A small revolver with a single bullet, though errant in its way, inescapable in its pursuit, found one man dead. One man dead and one pair of handcuffs. One brother who could not break out of jail and one who could not break in. Shag Wragrum became a lifer and his brother, the touch upon him yet, became a priest. They had gone out of the house one day, as their mother watched from her high window, and each had gone his own way, one up Ferrin Street and one down Ferrin Street in the heart of Charlestown, the wide sea around them closing in at the docks, and the stars proposing, setting demands.

Improper Burial at the First Iron Works of America

W ith one glass eye and with one wooden leg, but with a shovel in his hands, seventy-two-year-old Napoleon deMars was an earth surgeon. But he felt cold and clammy when his long handled shovel painstakingly pried up the buried object. It was disinterment! White of bone came at him, from the grave. It was a human skull, opened at a wedge in the frontal lobe, and Napoleon knew it most likely had been murder. The skull, and apparently some of its bones holding on to the last known form, lay at the end of his half day's work, a trench at the First Iron Works of America, in Saugus, a mere dozen miles from Boston's Freedom Trail. The site was being excavated for and from history. It was September of 1952. Excavation had been under way since 1948, on a small scale, but steady. Not a single piece of diesel-driven power equipment had been allowed in there as yet. It was a pick and shovel site, a whiskbroom site, toothpick and cotton swab country.

Now it was a graveyard.

Napoleon, for all his years, for all his toted calamities, felt nauseous.

Three people of varying importance were at the Iron Works site when the grisly discovery was made: Napoleon deMars, the seventy-two year old, one-eyed, one-legged earth surgeon; Dr. Roland Wells Dobbins, site archeologist who had found the ruins of Thoreau's cabin at Walden Pond a few years earlier, now in charge of unearthing the site of the very first iron works that had brought to America all the experience Europe was able to muster back in the 1600s; and Silas Tully, police officer of the town, on the force only a matter of six years after his service in the Marine Corps in the once-noisy Pacific.

On that high-blue September day, clouds lain over someplace else, the faintest breath of salt coming off the river, at eleven o'clock in the morning, Napoleon deMars put down his shovel. It was a half-hour to lunchtime and he never stopped work, he never cursed his place in life, he never gave cause to any boss. Here at the Iron Works, at $2.35 an hour and the best wage he had ever gotten, where he often thought that he could shovel until he was eighty, he put his work aside.

He looked out over the First Iron Works of America, up off the banks of the Saugus River on the North Shore above Boston. The site was a conglomeration of excavations, mounds, slag piles, marked stone walls which had been retrieved from history, a half dozen trenches cutting across a small piece of Saugus crooked as lightning, ragged as crossword puzzles, and the scattered piles of artifacts yet to be catalogued and put away.

Napoleon walked up the site with the marked limp he had carried with him for more than half a century. The broad band of a suspender hooked over one shoulder and slipped into his belt line where, down inside his pants, it connected to the crude wooden leg he had worn for so long. In reality, this one was his third, and no lighter than the first. Around the site he looked for Rollie Dobbins, boss man, a little prissy Napoleon had often thought, but more knowledgeable than any man in town on this kind of an excavation. Often enough he'd seen the light go on in Rollie's eyes when a new discovery was made, when a ditch gave up clues or artifacts, when the 17th Century struggled up out of a pile of dirt or the bottom of a hole like a woodchuck checking the lay of the land.

Now, Napoleon had found this new discovery. With effort he tried to reach back into history the way Rollie did. Long had he marveled at how much Rollie could pull out of a small find, the way a rock sat on its neighbor or what it was made of or how the demarcation in a trench of the natural soil line could tell time as good as a calendar.

Napoleon used his head to signal Rollie, as if giving signals to his dog, and nodded to his current digging spot.

Roland Wells Dobbins, dark-haired, round faced, handsome in his ruddy outdoors way, just now beginning to widen at the belt line a bit, tipped dark-rimmed glasses off his face and looked at Napoleon. From long standing he admired the old man, who kept his shovel moving more industriously than any two of the other laborers. Napoleon was also a good luck talisman for Rollie, his charm piece. He remembered the day he had hired the old man, who began methodically shoveling his way through three hundred years of fill. His single eye was a marvelously good organ. A cannon ball popped off his shovel that first day; a half dozen clay pipe remnants (with one bowl intact) turned up an hour later, on the second day the crusted remains of a matchlock pistol were held in the air just as the crew broke for lunch. For that one moment Rollie the archeologist had palmed devilish antiquity.

"What is it, Napoleon?" Sweat was a dark stain on Napoleon's shirt under the one-strap suspender. An off-yellow color it was, almost like an old tobacco stain, and made Rollie think of his grandfather for the first time in many years.

"Where I'm digging, boss. Down where you sent me yesterday to trench out. There's a skeleton." The old man's one eye had a remoteness in it. "It's in the fill. It's in some clay. I don't think I hit it with my shovel, but the front of the skull has been crushed. I didn't tell any of the others. It must have been a nasty death." A story wagged deep behind his one eye, his brow leaning over it darkly.

Rollie looked at his watch, smiled at Napoleon. "Thanks, Napoleon. Tell the others they can go for lunch. I'll check it out myself." Down the slope Rollie's gait was deliberate, drawing no eyes.

Down into the trench Napoleon had cut he eased himself. A neatness came at him immediately; the floor of the trench was level, the five foot sides were cut down as if they had been carved or sculpted out of the sand and gravel and blue-gray hardpan. The pile thrown out humped a long mound stretching away from the trench. The neat trench itself was about eighteen feet long. Beneath him he saw the bones of the skeleton Napoleon had unearthed. The skull indeed was crushed in at the forehead. Arm bones and torso bones had been exposed. A quick little chill spun on Rollie's skin and danced off someplace. Never before in any of his digs had he seen this. There'd been pots and pans and rocks and stones and clay pipes and glass bottles of every sort and pieces of wood with enough left of their grain that stories could still be extracted from them. But never the hard remains of a human being, just the subtle remains, the storied remains, never the boned and final remains.

The other workers thought it odd that Rollie and Napoleon during lunch had quickly set up a canvas tent over the trench. They hadn't seen a tent on-site in almost a year. It was, obviously, now out of bounds for them.

The third party on the scene, a daily visitor to the site, was Officer Silas Tully of the Saugus Police Department. For a couple of years he had watched as Rollie Dobbins pieced together so much of the original site from piles of rock and slag heaps and baskets full of artifacts, and now wondered what a tent signified. Curious, he made his way down to the tent, stepping over trenches with his long legs, jumping over small piles of slag or rocks, avoiding larger holes and pits. Rollie and he had become, if not friends, at least daily conversationalists on the topic of excavation. Each loved the way details and mysteries worked on them and each found in the other a sense of mirror. The particulars of each calling worked resolutely.

Si Tully slipped aside the canvas door flap of the tent and stepped inside. Rollie looked up at him from the bottom of the trench, a nonplused look on his face as if a policeman was absolutely the last person he wanted on site. With some effort Rollie climbed the ladder out of the trench. Touching the blue sleeve of Silas' shirt, a pained look, as if he had been surprised at the cookie jar or caught peeking in the girls' bathroom, flooded his face. In the hanging light of a Coleman lamp buzzing its ignition as noisy as bees his face reddened deeply.

"Si, we just can't let too many people in on this until we found out what it's all about!" His eyes affected beseeching. "They'll trample the hell out of the place. It'd take us months to recover. We can't let strangers in here."

"Find out what's what all about?" Silas said, and then, swiftly directed, he looked along the length of Rollie's arm pointing at the skull in the bottom of the trench, its forehead obviously crushed at a point of history.

Six years on the force and this was Si Tully's first skull and, moreover, his first skeleton. Bodies he'd seen, that's for sure, in the islands on the turnpike at crash scenes, laid out on the median strips more times than he cared to remember. This, though, was a new mystery to him; an unknown, a victim how long in the historic grave no one knew or might never know. Something told him that Rollie had made assessments, that one or more leads had already surfaced, that this gruesome crime would be solved. It was second nature to the archeologist. This could be most interesting, a bizarre and intriguing find at the archeological site, more than history unfurling itself.

Si spoke again. "It's my town, Rollie, and it's murder clear as a bell, and I've got to report it. You know that. No matter how old it is." The former Marine, the military man, early in this new episode, could see lines being crossed, basic command structure being aborted.

Rollie had seen the quizzical light in Silas' eyes before. Again he touched him on the arm. This time it was as if he were drawing the young policeman into a strictest confidence; the secret of King Tut's tomb, a hidden room beneath the Sphinx, a new Rosetta Stone unearthed in old Yankee Saugus. Consciously he decided not to tell Silas of the other waiting discovery; there *were* stars to be earned! The pirate Treach had paved the way.

Rollie stood beside the trench looking down at the skeleton, down where history was always telling him stories. A storyteller might have been reciting the sad and gruesome tale to him, a tale of love turned sour, of madness, a tale of clandestine deeds performed or perpetrated under cover of darkness. In the air he could feel hatred, and despair. A man, he thought, a seaman perhaps, had come home from the high angry seas only to find more trouble at the hearth. His mind kept telling him it had a will of its own, despite the training, the years of experience. Mystery, he knew, did it. But, he thought with some eagerness, he lived on mysteries.

Rollie still held Silas by the arm, working on the mystery, the love of details in the policeman which made his own life go 'round. "I'm going to get Professor Hartley out here from Harvard. Loves this place he does and he'll love this challenge. I can see him marshaling the forces at Harvard, getting his cronies in the labs to do us a few favors. His forensic friends will have a small busman's holiday on this, their own little murder to play with. They'll love it, the boys of the old school, in a deep, dark secret, rolling up their pant legs and getting down and dirty. They'll give us the answer to every question we can come up with, you and I. Then, with it all laid out, you can go to the chief or the State or whoever else and lay a clean solved case right on the blotter." There was affirmation in his eyes, in his voice.

He squeezed Silas' arm. They were standing there on the edge of history. It could have been The Valley of Kings under their feet, or Chitzen-itsa, or a Ming Dynasty tomb somewhere in China. Again he squeezed Silas' arm, brothers of the mystery.

Early Sunday morning two station wagons rolled into the parking area of the Iron Works. Rollie and Silas met Professor D'Jana K. Hartley—tall, effectively studious-looking in his tweed leathered elbows, but not in a boring way—and his cohorts from the ivy halls—two more archeologists; a forensic expert and his young sidekick with blond hair and extremely bright eyes; a professor of Humanities who looked to be the most intelligent of all; a man who carried from the trunk of one car a canvas bag of assorted gear; and a young good looking woman wearing denim, boots, and a yellow blouse fitting her so well that most others would not believe she was from Harvard. None of the site diggers, that's for sure, noting how compelling yellow was.

Napoleon deMars watched them approach. Leaning on his shovel near the tent, he was still on the clock, still at $2.35 an hour, and no one, not one soul, had entered the tent since he'd received his orders from Rollie. Perhaps the victim was as old as he was, perhaps a person he had known in his youth. His mind went skipping back through the years for a noted loss. Nothing came to mind. Napoleon watched the Harvards at work and admired the deftness of their hands with the small trowels and brushes they employed, yet was certain the soft leather boots they wore must have cost a week's pay. He tried to hear the whispers and small asides that connected them, made them such outlanders down in the hole he had cut into the earth.

Professor D'Jana Hartley's crew were crack specialists. Quietly they went their turn back into the minor history of the skeleton in the trench of the Iron Works. Small talk amongst them, as much whisper as anything could be, as if covering a trail of a known confidant, had scanned a series of possibilities: an indentured servant, probably a Scot, a slag toter or bog digger or barrow pusher, who had fallen astray, perhaps with another slave's woman or the Iron Master's wife, and they tittered at a remark about a new ax of Cane manufactured on the very spot and which had done the improbable deed; a late visitor to the site, pocketbook or pouch laden with crown coin or Spanish gold pieces, fallen under the swing of a metal bar, come slowly as an ingot of first life out of the very furnace whose ruins lay at their backs, in the hands of another indentured servant waiting to buy his way out of contract.

Now and then a giggle caught itself on the tall air. Napoleon, intently watching every move, hearing every sound, thought of his grandchildren at the cookie jar and smiled at the likeness of things. He'd work till ninety if they let him, and if the other leg would hold its own, here in this affable cradle of history. On the way home he'd buy a box of cookies for the cookie jar; it was a fair swap.

The dig, though, was a Chinese checkerboard of ups and downs, holes and trenches and piles and mounds of earth, almost a battle zone of sorts. The slag pile looked like it might have oozed out of the place where Rollie had said the furnace originally was. It was twenty feet high or thereabouts and ran towards the river for ninety or more feet. When the sun caught a slick side of slag, like a shiny piece of coal with an enamel surface, one would think of a semaphore signal leaping from darkness. The land sloped away from the Iron Master's House on the high point to where the salt water reached at high tide, a good two miles and a half up the Saugus River from the Atlantic Ocean, itself a trove of history. Legend had it that a pirate captain, Treach or Langton perhaps, had brought his ship a good way up the river and then landed a long boat further up, a boat which had carried much of his plunder to be buried in Dungeon Rock, now a huge hole 135 feet down in solid rock and bare miles away in the Lynn Woods Reservation.

The young policeman, at the same time, was not standing still. A minor conviction had told him that the skeleton was not too old; at least, not of Colonial age. This conviction he accepted as coming from an intelligence and a feel for things that he had cultivated while on the job and while in the military. Immediately he had gone to a retired postman, a neighbor of his for years, who was a veritable historian of the town, gossip or rumor or fact. Silas had found out that the stagecoach road from Boston to Newburyport had, at one time, run right past the backside of the Iron Works. That, too, was on what was now Central Street. That Central Street, still clear in Silas' mind, had once swept right on by the front of the Iron Works. Somewhere in town, a long time ago, but not as long as some might think it, a person had disappeared, or had been murdered, or had been buried in the lap of history. Silas Tully made his mind up that he was going to solve this case; that he would find out whose bones had been buried at the Iron Works.

The weekly *Saugus Advertiser* and the *Lynn Daily Evening Item* seemed to be his best choices and he began a one-man search for a person who had suddenly gone unaccounted for. Through reams and reams of old copies he labored. To old time reporters and editors he talked and in turn haunted the cracker barrels and barroom back rooms and sundry other locations they had directed him to. These were places where history walked, where history talked, where the tongues of history carried on the legends and the lineage that might never make its way into print. Over-the-fence stuff. Dark alley stuff. Stories he never heard before surfaced, debris riding up on the tide, swollen drains dumping pieces of the town into the river, silt of lives streaming away. Old copies of Saugus *Gazette* and Saugus *Herald* and *Lynn Transcript*, Lynn being the next being town over, to the east, brought nothing to light. No headlines, no want ads for a lost person, no missing person with no single accounting. No melodramas in the local library of a missing girl or boy or a triangle affair gone haywire.

But he was resolute.

It was *Ars Veritas* that brought things into focus after Rollie's discovery of the coin.

An informal, unsigned, handwritten report came to Rollie Dobbins a mere three days after the Harvard entourage had first hit the Iron Works. Line by line, item by item, he considered the information set forth:

The subject is male, thirty-one years of age, dead of a savage blow to the frontal lobe of the skull. Death was immediate. It is estimated that he has been covered since mid year of 1905. His watch stopped at 2:17 of a day, in the a.m. we would assume, and was German, a Gersplank, very limited in production and rarely seen this side of the Atlantic. He carried a small sum of coin. One leg, the right, was 3/4 inch shorter than the other. He had been an accident victim prior to his demise, his hip and thigh bone both having been fractured, the right side, and most likely about two years prior to his end. He was perhaps in military uniform at the time of his death, as determined by tunic buttons found at the site, an officer of a captain's rank, United States Cavalry, 22nd Regiment Massachusetts. No military identification was found on-site, which we find questionable and suspicious in nature, inasmuch as his pouch was neither emptied nor removed. Two bones in right index and right middle finger were broken, which we assume to have happened at or close to the scene of discovery, at time of death, meaning struggle. A length of chain had been dropped or had fallen onto the body and was found, remains of it, rusted solid on top of the spinal column. No other objects or material were found in proximity of the remains except for a small figure of jade of unknown origin discovered a mere two feet from the left hand, the figure tending towards Chinese but not yet confirmed, but probably pre-Ming.

In summation we offer the following: Victim was a thirty-one-year-old professional military man with healed bone fractures of hip and leg and was probably in uniform at death but must have been on a limited duty roster; did struggle at time of death as evidenced by broken fingers but was mortally wounded and died immediately from severe trauma to forehead. May have had Chinese or Far East connection, if indeed the jade piece found nearby does not prove to be Incan or pre-Incan. Our camp is exactly halved on this last point.

The lack of any evidence of fabric, other than his pouch, gathers suspicion the more we think about it, especially concerning tunic buttons and no tunic residue of note. It is possible that his uniform was biodegradable and has passed on, but we doubt that. Therefore we think he may have been nude (stripped under duress) and pushed bodily into a hole. If he was nude, the evidence of tunic buttons indicates they may have been placed there to mislead any subsequent authority inquest, and we must ask why. Certainly, the person who committed this deed did not expect it to be discovered in the foreseeable future, but was covering tracks for any discovery some years down the road. It therefore causes us to think he was known to the victim, was himself in the military, tried to put sand in the gears (so to speak), or, as D'Jana Hartley said on last resort, it was a military man who killed a civilian and tried to thwart any future identification by throwing in the tunic buttons, like the proverbial hand of gravel as in dust unto dust, probably off his own shirt, a kindly killer who took the shirt off his own back.

We have a worldwide network working on the jade figure and feel that it was indeed a portion of loot from some local robbery. We shall keep you advised as to all incoming information or any changes in our collective thinking. In close proximity to the remains was found a 1903 one cent piece, but we do not know if this coin was interred with the remains or had later fallen into the hole during excavation.

Archeologist Rollie Dobbins, giggling at much of the report, found the humor effective, the conclusions as palpable as his own, and, for the most part, felt the mystery deepen.

Saugus patrolman, and armchair detective when he had to be or needed to be, Silas Tully, at receiving the report and the information on the 1903 cent, found his new starting point and went right to it. For no reason apparent to himself, he gave a grace year to the passage of time, skipped 1904 and went right to 1905. 1905, it appeared, after much scrutinizing of papers and books and magazines and other information almanacs, was the year of the Russians, or, as he quipped to himself, the year the Russias didn't do too well. The Japs whipped their butt all over hell in their war; they lost 200,000 in the Mukden battle alone, had their naval fleet destroyed in the Strait of Tsushima, lost Sakhalin Island outright, got badly overrun in Manchuria, and a number of other places. Crewmen of the great battleship *Potemkin* mutinied and eventually turned the ship over to Rumanian authorities. The Russian Grand Duke, Sergei Aleksandrovich, the uncle of Czar Nicholas II, was assassinated by a bomb thrown into his lap by a revolutionary. The Russian pot certainly was stirring and much of the world was in turmoil, and, of course, he realized, being on this side of the information trail one could see to where a lot of all this was leading.

A few other events attracted his eye, disparate events, no obvious ties between them, but events that rode on top of tidal debris, like cheese boxes or pieces of flotsam, bobbing to be noticed: the Cullinan Diamond, all 3,106 carats of it, was discovered in Transvaal and insurance underwritten by a U.S. company; the body of American Naval hero John Paul Jones was found in a cemetery in Paris and was moved to the United States, perhaps in a cask of rum for a preservation attempt; the Russo-Japanese War was ended by a pact signed practically in Saugus' own back yard, at Portsmouth, New Hampshire, after a key role was played by the old stick-swinger himself, President Teddy Roosevelt, and closer to home, just a few miles away, the palatial home of W. Putnam Wesley, on the Saugus-Wakefield line in what had become the Breakheart Reservation, was robbed in the dead of night by an unknown male who threatened three servants with bodily harm or death if they tried to escape from a pantry they had been locked into, chopping off a butler's finger with an old sword to prove his vow.

Silas Tully went to sleep that night after chewing all these things over in his mind, locked in on all the international stuff he knew he was out of his element. But down deep something fervent told him he was going along for the whole ride. All the way. And a bare thread of light, the thinnest lisle possible, gossamer at best, seemed to be pulling at these disparate events.

Upon W. Putnam Wesley he settled for his first stepping-stone towards a solution. Filthy rich to say the least, much of it come by way of his grandfather from the California gold fields and parlayed by his father, Wesley had various shades of darkness sitting around him. He had journeyed far and wide, especially in Europe and the Far East, often with a large entourage. His interest included, after money, artifacts of historical intrigue (such as dueling swords or dueling pistols from famous encounters), *objects d'art* tending to explicit sex of any selection, gems so special that there might not have been a match with another, all things Chinese that might be described by one or more of the aforementioned. He had had four wives, three of whom died in the midst of a long trip or voyage. Silas found one report of his fourth wife having taken a shot at him, in jest as they declared. Silas figured the threat of that single shot to have saved her life.

Wesley was called Puttee from his earliest days, both from his middle name and from his adventurous youthful habit, when playing soldier games, of wearing strips of cloth which circled his legs from ankle to knee, much in the manner of real soldiers. His name he wore well.

The sixth sense was working overtime for Silas a few days later when he sat with Rollie under a tarp at the Iron Works site. They discussed their points of view and all the data of the *Ars Veritas* report.

"It's a crime of passion," Rollie finally affirmed, his voice steady, convincing in its stoic way, his dark serious eyes looking out over the site and seeing, oblivious to Silas Tully, what the site would eventually look like. His baby, Rollie's baby, put to bed.

"A marriage is involved," he continued, "a triangle affair. I think we must look to the Hawkridges. Powerful, money by the handfuls, owners of the site for a long time, their papers still scattered throughout the Iron Master's house like they've just gone away for the weekend and will be back on Monday to square things away."

He seemed to mull over his own words before he added, "Perhaps the Hawkridges were so powerful that the absence of one of the family could easily be explained."

"You've found something?" Silas said, turning to face Rollie as they sat on a fence rail. The light in Rollie's eyes was amber, obvious. Silas, from day one of their acquaintance, knew that Rollie's bent was to the romantic, to the clandestine, Rollie's eye having that other light in them.

"Yes," Rollie said. "One of the Hawkridges, Carlton Theophus Hawkridge. About thirty years of age that I know of. Went off on a trip somewhere around 1905, perhaps a bit later, and was never heard from again."

"How do you know that?"

"From a few letters I found in a box in the upper rooms. Went off supposedly very quickly on a trip for his health. Not the most likable fellow, not from what I gather, but *family*."

"Do you think the family did him in?" Si's eyes were deep with question, his scowl like punctuation.

"I really don't know that, but we scrambled at the beginning of all this to go a lot further back than we thought we could. "What have you come up with?"

As though he expected no reply, Rollie looked away from Silas, seeing the sun catch on the water of the river, an angular slicing of light in the late afternoon, sometimes gold, sometimes blue, that leaped across the river and onto Vinegar Hill where he just knew Treach's treasure was buried. The hole being dug he could picture, the chest being lowered, the rocks being piled up. He could see the descent of the crew back down to the longboat, could see their soft and easy float down the river to the ship shifting slightly at anchor. He knew where his next job was coming from. And if the skeleton in the trench was one Carlton Theophus Hawkridge, or could safely assumed to be so, the move to the next dig would be a cinch.

So much depended on the young policeman sitting beside him. Spoon feeding him would be a challenge. Subtle as a snake it would need to be.

Silas Tully gave nothing away. Not even the fact that he knew he was not a rank amateur, that knots in spite of all apparent were being slowly tied, that the gossamer thread would come to rope. If Roland Dobbins had his blind romance, he had his own.

"I just keep poking along, Rollie, trying to tie things together. It's all so far away, as if never touching us with reality."

"If it's Hawkridge, Si, I can see a spread in the Boston papers for you. Perhaps a magazine article. You could turn this old Yankee town right up on its ear! They'll be beating a path to your door. You couldn't beat them off." His smile was broader than a shovel blade. And the shovel blade was slicing deep into a pile of manure.

"The Japanese tried that, Rollie. It didn't work for them either."

There was a declaration he hoped Rollie would understand. Edging off the fence rail, he waved slightly, almost half-heartedly. "I'll keep you posted, Rollie. You do the same." There was another one.

As Si walked off, Rollie looked out over the site, saw a glancing shaft of light leap off the river and leap up to the crest of Vinegar Hill. Treach just knew he was coming after him! Bet on it!

The gossamer thickened indeed later that week for Silas Tully. An article in an old issue of a discontinued Boston paper, about Old Ironsides and the Charlestown Navy Yard, tied together John Paul Jones and W. Putnam "Puttee" Wesley. It was a single line implying that the container bringing home the body of the hero was used to illegally convey some priceless artifacts. And Puttee Wesley was accompanying the body home, a service he so graciously volunteered to perform, inasmuch as he was in Paris and on his way home. President Roosevelt accepted the offer. The thin line of gossamer, with a little more body to it, seemed to fall like a shadow of netting on the piece of jade that had lain so long in the earth beside another body.

Silas had come to abrupt attention, as if the old Commander-in-Chief himself had walked in on him. Life was full of little pieces of goodness. Find them, that's all you had to do. They were at your feet, in your back pocket, around the corner.

Puttee Wesley, he decided from all that he ingested of him, was not afraid of playing either the pirate or the brigand or the smuggler to get any of the items his heart desired. If money wouldn't buy them, he'd get them one way or another. In 1919 he had died suddenly, unprotected by his money or his treasures, from a bout with influenza. The family then, as many families do under pressure, had scattered, their fortunes wasted, and little evidence of Puttee Wesley's existence hung on. Breakheart had become pond and forest and a scattering of trails, the huge mansion gone to ground, a bare bit of stone foundation thrusting out of brush. But to Silas there came echoes repeating themselves like gunshots down between canyon walls, the continuing onslaught of the same notion, all these things, Jones and Puttee and the jade piece and the skeleton, were caught up in the same web, the same gossamer spinning out of his mind, spinning out of the twist of all the years.

Rollie Dobbins had tried to plumb Silas' mind a number of times, tried to steer him to the Hawkridges, but fell short with each attempt. The stubbornness of the young policeman, though a craggy veteran, bothered him more than he let on.

Treach had waited this long, but he might not wait forever. Even in death the pirate might be a most rambunctious ghost.

It took a strange turn of events to swing matters in the correct direction, the kind of luck that Silas Tully knew would come of endless scratching, endless probing, endless digging, his own *l'affair archeology.* If his French were much better he'd be able to spell it right.

It was a naval clerk at the Pentagon who remembered Silas Tully's numerous inquiries about the John Paul Jones transfer, who had seen Silas' letter concerning the suspicions surrounding the hero's remains being brought home, who a long time earlier in his current assignment had begun reading old documents in the Navy archives.

Seaman First Class Peter J. Leone wrote the following to Officer Silas Tully of the Saugus Police Department:

This is not an official document and is only sent to you on a personal basis because of the interest you have excited in me about the Admiral John Paul Jones situation. I have come across a number of old documents and communiqués concerning the Admiral's coming home to where he should have been. If there is anything else I might furnish, I will try, but I think you will be interested in what has caught my eye in the files. The president at the time, Theo. Roosevelt, was advised of certain shady deals that might be attached to the movement of the Admiral's remains. The information came in a letter to him from a Bruce Jacob Bellbend, a captain in British intelligence, who had accidentally come on the information while on a separate assignment. It did mention illegal movement of precious artifacts that had been taken from unknown sources. The president assigned a personal representative, Captain Arthur G. Savage, U.S. Navy, to proceed to Paris and accompany the remains home and to investigate and report to him any and all findings he might come across. None of the captain's reports are in file, but I did find the following information about him: he was from Grand Hawk, Minnesota, was a graduate of the Naval Academy, was captain of the U.S.S. Standish at one time, did suffer a serious accident aboard ship that required medical leave (hip and leg injury in a fall, right side), had a deep scar on his left cheek of unknown cause, was a gutsy and devoted leader of men, and loved nothing better than his country. He was reported as being missing in July of 1905 and nothing more is known of him, as though he had gone off the face of the Earth.

Silas Tully brought his case to rest, though it lay at his feet for a few days, being stepped on, turned over, cemented back into place. He could see Puttee Wesley or one of his henchmen knock the captain on the head, take him under cover of darkness to where Central Street was being filled in, dropping him in the hole, throwing on top of his bare body the buttons of some army tunic to throw leads elsewhere in case the body might be discovered. The jade piece, still unidentified, was sacrificed to help the scattering of leads. The remnants of chain continued to be nothing more than a corrosive coil in his mind. The precious artifacts put away for the time being.

Silas Tully told it all to his wife Phyllis and none of it to Rollie Dobbins.

Napoleon deMars, with the help of two grandchildren and two sons-in-law, held sway over the tent for another week until the remains of the unknown body, as it was officially treated, were laid quietly to further rest in a shaded area of Riverside Cemetery, just outside of Saugus Center, alongside the railroad tracks no longer in use.

One evening thereafter, Rollie Dobbins, maverick archeologist, ramrod of stones and bones, continued to watch the late afternoon sun glance off the river with surprising richness. Flares of light flew like spears, shy sparks reigned as though diamonds had been loosed from chest or pouch. Gallant red wing blackbirds from both sides of the river flew across and through shafts of late light like arrows onto their targets. Dusk, as part of shadow, settled itself softly, a dust, atop the colonial town. Vinegar Hill and Round Hill and Hemlock Hill and Indian Slide and dark passages of Breakheart Reservation shifted into the shadows that history continually lends to its constituents. Treach had such a night, he was sure. And he was out there, his subtle remains, waiting for him in those shadows.

And one night a few weeks later, when all was quiet, the sky a dark canopy, Silas Tully, a policeman always, a Marine forever, a patriot feeling the pains of wounds he had long forgotten, his eyes raw with sadness, thinking of the admiral and the captain and the president and the seaman at the Pentagon, knowing the town he loved would cement the ultimate resolve, affixed above that single grave at the Veteran's Section of Riverside Cemetery a wooden sign he had carved one long night filled with the deepest of thoughts. It read: *ARTHUR G. SAVAGE, CAPTAIN U.S. NAVY, WHO DIED IN THE SERVICE OF HIS COUNTRY.*

There would be no fanfare, no clarions or trumpets or drums. No gunfire. The captain would sift into the past, along with all the other veterans from all the other wars, all the warriors the town had ceded to history. He'd have a flag atop his grave on Memorial Day, put there by the American Legion. The breeze and the sunlight would catch at it, flapping it about. Children would wave back. A few seniors, offering up their own kinds of parades, would offer serious nods. The wind would come back again and again, a rapture of touch, a salute of sorts. Nights would accept the continual silence abounding in Riverside.

Silas Tully thought he could give Captain Arthur Savage nothing more precious than that.

When he told his wife, she loved him all over again.

The Puzzle Solution's Swift Shift from Irony

A man in a black suit rides the train to work every day and doesn't talk to anybody because he's been trying to solve a puzzle for seven years and is frustrated by his predicament.

For seven long years, at least by his count, Creighton Manning, architect and music lover, had been trying to solve a puzzle on a morning train ride to his job in the city. Finally, he relented and began thinking of it as his seven-year itch, knowing what it was doing to him, but not what it had done to him. That itch, though, had worn him down, and he had, in turn, been passed over for promotion during those years, and just as casually ignored by other people. But contentment, he understood with a grain of reality, comes in strange shapes, often keeps strange company.

Neat in dress, rarely noticeable in any larger-than-usual gathering, his steady move into anonymity did not bother him. Creighton was clean in habit, healthy, and bought a new suit every ten months, giving his oldest one to a charity collection; this action, inside of a year's time, was a sign of contented affluence with him. On Saturday evenings he shined his three pairs of dress shoes while listening to his favorite opera or one of his classical musical composites, or, now and then, watching an old black and white mystery film. There were moments during such films that, with his eyes closed and concentrating on the music, he would be able to "see" the action, swore he could script it, could put Dick Powell

51

without a song or Grade-B Chester Morris's Boston Blackie into an appropriate atmosphere.

This morning was a morning like all others; he collected his newspaper and his decaf coffee at the variety store less than a block from the train station, now elegantly squeezed in between two much taller but artless buildings. His black leather briefcase bounced at one knee. He carried no umbrella, though he found the sky dreary and gray and believed the smell of rain sat in the air, a kind of immovable notification. With that mindset, he studied the leaves on tree and bush and saw their attitudes fully in place. The thirsty would drink when needed, he acknowledged, and, reflecting on his own schedule, did not hurry his steps. Timing for train departure was ingrained in him, posed all around him in varying evidence: the silent and sometimes erratic clock on the classic Georgian church tower was there; and the bells over at the Wellborne Grade School; and the village bus, with a puff of smoke and sounding as if its pistons were abrading each other, would start abruptly on schedule for its run up to Mt. Hebron Village.

Ultimately, as if driven by an internal primal clock, there was Jake Manther the house builder coming back home at seven-thirty on the button every morning, supposedly for coffee with his wife Corine, but everybody knew the kids had gone to school for the day, all four of them. Creighton had heard it said that if Corine worked a pillow the way she walked, even down the grocery aisle, it was no wonder Jake was faithful and punctual. Creighton had never seen Corine in the grocery store, though he had once seen her standing in line at the post office in that sort of provocative one-legged stance some women have mastered. Once he had uttered the term "hip thruster," he never let it go. Corine was a "hip thruster." Occasionally that observation made his throat dry.

Creighton sat in the last seat in the first car, where he had sat practically every workday for the seven years he'd spent at Carmody, Halliburton & Sands, Architects of Note. Oh, how he loved the inside joke of that title and had composed a little music for it that not one other person in the world had any knowledge of. None of the other passengers, many of them along for the same ride to the city for work, paid much attention to him, or to his occasional whistle, except for conceding Creighton his usual seat. Other than a cursory nod, they had conceded that seat long ago. None of passengers knew about Creighton's puzzle, which he would set up on his briefcase as soon as everybody was seated. This ascertainment was not seen, not heard, but felt; he never looked up fearing someone, at discovery, would be looking into his eyes, as if the puzzle would be reflected there.

The puzzle was his alone to decipher, his alone. He whistled softly at his work, the whistle saying where he was, what he was at. When the music went wrong, Halliburton hit a bad note, he'd put the puzzle away.

On the upside the puzzle appeared to be a common crossword puzzle, but it had never come out right, had never been solved by the interminable architect. He had delved into huge dictionaries, gone through strange adaptations found in the dictionary from the Latin and the French, and those sly, short mouthfuls of words without vowels from the Welsh like "cwm" and "crwth." Nothing he tried ever fit two exasperating corners of the puzzle. Nothing at all!

In his architect's mind, the plot plan of blank and solid squares came scribed and burned into his cerebrum. It was there, he would swear, immediately behind his forehead, swearing that any minute it might broadcast itself across his brow. With those blank and solid black squares he could tile a whole bathroom. It would be a snap. And with a clarity he found unfathomable, he could close his eyes, see the puzzle on a sheet of mechanical drawing paper on his high school desk and feel old Mr. Bund looking over his shoulder, grading his work, though Mr. Bund's words were lost from memory. What would that long-gone teacher of isometric drawings have to say about a lineal puzzle? There was more than one simple mystery abounding.

Once, Creighton said to himself that he could scribe the graphic and text of the puzzle without a miss, and could do it in fifteen minutes. He had worn words and pencils down to their nubs, made copy after copy of the puzzle. At times, he knew its clutches were rhythmic and constant, like a piece of music had been tapped into his brain, as though a piece of nostalgic music was at once known and unknown. Yet there was absolutely nothing auricular about his puzzle, no word spoken, no huff or puff of breath at annunciation. His puzzle was mated with silence.

Melanie, his wife, on about the fourth year, having seen the incomplete puzzle on a number of occasions, like falling out of an inner pocket from one of his suit coats, or scattered in his jewelry drawer like quaint intruders, finally asked him about the rote he was apparently caught up in.

"Creighton, I swear I've seen this same puzzle at least a dozen times. It's never done. Can't you finish it? Can I help?" They were watching a Thin Man movie.

God forbid, he thought. Not after all of this. "It's but a game, Melanie. Like notes out of place and you're positive you know the score, but it eludes you. No, no great importance, dear. I while my time away with it, but only on the train. It's easier than watching the backsides of houses or clothes hanging on porches or on clotheslines like sails trying for the wind, or seeing how long one deserted Buick can stay in one place for years on end." That, he figured, would put her off the track.

She had picked up the newspaper after he had shined his shoes and folded it and placed it in the wastebasket. "If ever," she said, and went back to William Powell with his hair never out of place, his suit immaculate, and his grin too sly to be real. The puzzle was not mentioned again by her, as if it had been blown away in the wind mere as an October leaf.

Creighton closed down on his seventh year with the puzzle, ultimately content with knowing he had something to do on the train ride both ways, that life had certain promises and perils, and that time had dictates all its own. Continuity would go on until you met a wall or you fell off somewhere. There was the simplicity; his puzzle was shrouded in silence. The true words might never be spoken. He never saw the derelict Buick chained onto a truck bed to be hauled away, only once had forgotten into the eleventh month about buying another suit, and closed that fault in a hurry. He always felt a flurry of joy when Halliburton came perfectly from his lips regardless who was about him, even at the office.

The peak of frustration in Creighton Manning's odyssey comes the night, late for one train, early for the next one, he drops into a small cafe to have a drink. Daringly, time floating in the air, the puzzle forgotten for the moment, he decides on Scotch, which he hasn't touched for years. He is aware of subtle change hanging on the edges.

Two older men at the bar, both bearded and a bit crusty, holding beer bottles in their hands like handles of bayonets, are talking about the time when they were in the Marine Corps, in another country with a Marine Legation. Creighton hears how they as editors used to make up crossword puzzles for the Legation's small mimeographed newspaper, and the first Marine in with the completed puzzle would get a bottle of whiskey. With their own bottle of whiskey, the two editors used to lock themselves in the squad tent that housed the company clerk's office and the newspaper office, and make up the paper and the crossword puzzle. Their guffaws are loud and boisterous, and they take turns in slapping the bar top. They laugh heartily and continually about a puzzle they'd made up once when they had been drinking heavily and there had been no winner and they couldn't solve the puzzle themselves when the whole Legation stormed the entrance to the squad tent and demanded the solution be made public.

That night Creighton Manning took a cab home.

Silent Retrieval

The day had a head start on young Liam Craddock, he could feel it, and all that it promised. Across the years, on the slimmest sheet of air, piggybacking a whole man's aura on that fleet thinness, he caught the sense of tobacco chaw, or toby, mule leather's hot field abrasion, gunpowder's trenchant residue, men at confusion. If it wasn't a battlefield in essence, or scarred battle ranks, he did not know what else it could be. And it carried the burning embers of memory.

The yellowed pages of a hand-written Civil War journal had fallen open at Liam's feet, almost 146 years since the first shot was fired in that war. The calligraphy grabbed at him first, faded in areas and yet sweeping with an old-line flourish making him wonder about the tone and meter of the language, sensing an initial presence of old-fashioned pompousness or posed dignity. Practically nudging it aside at its birth, he quickly discarded this hastily formed opinion. With deep interest pushing at him, coming from an unnamed and limitless source, he had been scrounging in the attic of the old farm house in Bow, New Hampshire, a long way from battle sites near Richmond in Virginia, Baker's Creek in Mississippi, or Shiloh or Spring Hill in Tennessee. For more than 125 of those years an arm of the Craddock family had lived here at Bow, in a colonial farmhouse with seven rooms, two huge chimneys, a hogback out back and wide fields out front, and riding up near hills like a lease extension. Now, just turned 20, a good looking student, wiry and athletic, dark Irish complexion possibly inherited from an early Spanish sailor overboard off Ireland's coast, Liam loved to read about the Civil War, anything he could get his hands on. It had settled into him, geared his interests like a smart gift, when he was young boy. And here, an unexpected present, was a first hand account, from his great great great-grandfather, Ronan Craddock, Sergeant, Company C, 43rd Georgia Infantry Regiment, Army of Tennessee.

The war was real for both of them, the writer and the reader, the crucible of unbelievable deaths, mounds of dead men, fields strewn with dead men, row on row of dead men, the smell of death floating uphill like a pot of evil at a boil. He cringed and came abreast of his courage again. And there, deep in his genes, complementary, he felt the tug of the sea where the rough tide had brought ashore the Spanish sailor his grandfather talked so often about, as if he himself had met that Armada seaman. "We have all been warriors," the old man said on many occasions, his pipe lit on the porch letting off an Edgeworth cut, a soft breeze whispering in the cornfields, "since that swimmer caught up a lass. And your turn will come, Liam, in one manner or another. You may never know the shape of its coming, but come it will, and bring you to conflict. If you never wear a uniform, you'll still be in the ranks."

It was promise more than omen, more legacy than habit, and had long settled in place. All this time the journal had been so close to him and yet so far. He wondered where his attention had been, if anybody left had known of the journal's existence. Then, in one flame of awareness, he was sure his grandfather knew of this "find," had seen it coming to him.

Awareness crammed him, knowing he nursed a brooding hunger about "things unusual." This was like other sensations coming home in his mind, taking deep root. Liam could feel the message coming toward him, almost ascribed, not as swift as a shot, but unerring in its aim. The stilted handwriting, dense in some places as if battlefield artifacts were in tow, or faded in others portions the way a sleepy hand might write, scrawled often with afterthoughts along the narrow margins, came alive and gave this readable account:

Lord, I believe it is 30ᵗʰ April, 1864. Wravel Grane died in these arms this day, from a minie ball lodged in his neck and tearing apart a huge vein profuse in bleeding. A gentle man he was, and dear friend and comrade, who never once let an alcoholic drink pass his lips. The man knew no curses, and if they had ever sounded in his head, he never once in my company managed them to use. His last words to me, of any personal approach, came on this bright dawn where we looked out on the Virginia countryside stretching before us a greaten and resplendent new birth of the land. As they did in Pickens County, back home in Georgia, forward slopes of hills proved quicker at greenery than backsides, but spreading fast, and maple's aroma swam full to the air. The sun struck all a goodly light the whole while.

Wravel and I were west of Richmond but few miles, in sight of the James River, and had but a canister of bread found in the trappings of a dead Union soldier, nearly at our feet toward sleep. His left eye and cheek were missing and made him grotesque so near to that dread sleep. Lt. Griggs said to kick him aside, kick that human instrument You used to grant us Your bread. Wravel had said earlier that You would provide for us. You did provide a burial place for him locally, after we received your bread. Lord, I thank You for that. As we scanned the far hills at dawn, smoke rising from a hundred positions, life moving ever on, Wravel came aware that certainties and grimalkins or Old Harry himself were piling atop him. "Do not get separated from me ever, Ronan," he had implored, in the awful goodness that was owed in him. Know all that Wravel's words haunt me yet, about that separation and know they ever will.

The last entry, in the inch-thick journal with dust as an extra cover, read: *I say Amen, Lord. I was wounded at Jonesboro,*

Georgia, 31st August 1864 and was at home on furlough, unfit for further service, at the close of the war, my fated comrade Wravel Grane so soon gone aground. Will You will a reunion?

In between those two entries, Ronan Craddock, of Company C, 43rd Georgia Infantry Regiment, Army of Tennessee, had been captured at Baker's Creek, Mississippi on 16th May 1863, exchanged at Port Delaware, Delaware, and re-entered the military. The above entry followed there in place and pulled Liam deeper into the mix, cocking his interest to a higher pitch, and penetrating him as deep as a bayonet wound.

He felt at odds with the world, as though its elements were plaguing him only. The autumn chill settled atop him, though smooth as a plastic cover. An October wind talked at the lone window, yet the dust on the hinged travel trunk appeared undisturbed for a long time. Whorls of dust were petals on the trunk lid, and the brass lock obviously had not been opened in years. For the next three hours, autumn's touch running its full gamut on him, day slowly falling beside him in another pile dim under bulb, Liam Craddock read every word written by Sgt. Ronan Craddock, of the Army of Tennessee. As far as Liam knew, Ronan was the first in a line of family soldiers *this side of Ireland and that other war.*

Excerpts of the journal were absolute horror shows on every page: about the death around the sergeant, who could count bodies and limbs at day's end separated by the hundreds and hundreds; who had seen headless men fall directly beside him on the skirmish line, their heads elsewhere unknown; who had seen dead men near dusk sitting horseback or astride a mule grazing among the bodies; who had seen his best friend come to a bloody pulp in a matter of seconds.

Liam's body would jerk uncontrollably at each of these descriptions of mortality, as though taste and smell and sound, and the awful forbidden touch, had found him company in the attic in a last stab of unearthly silence.

He was somehow surviving a horrible day.

At length, darkness full on him, his mind completely blown away by journal revelations, seeing Ronan Craddock practically come alive in a hundred scenes. Liam put the journal back into the trunk and closed the cover. A thumping kept time at his breast, bringing a hollow echo to the back of his head, the kind an empty canyon emits, a still room, a dark hallway. Ideas and approaches of every sort leaped upon him and he had to get away to sort all the efforts of his mind as they tried to tell him what to do, what path to take.

"Whoa, man, you are something else," he said at one point, dipping his head in solemn salute to that old patriarch of battle, whose war scenes, as full of life as though he had been there to experience them, kept crossing his mind swift as movie reruns. They banged out a code of conduct for night listening. Lines of march and deployment came to him, shadowy, at edges of the attic room. Campfires lit up darker corners, though shadows ran loose again. The rustle of a night at war triggered other visions right on the edge of certainty. The footsteps of a camp guard sounded faintly but surely in the midst of an otherwise eerie silence. Then, loose in the dusk of evening, a horse's hoofs tattled far whereabouts, a messenger in flight or a runaway. Gunfire residue rose as sharp as skunk odor on the air, cosmoline odor just as persistent. The senses amuck.

All the parts of war came as real as a brick in the hand, a wash of wind, the smell of flesh at discord.

Liam's father, Desmond, lone son of Padraig, in the line of lone sons back through Lucas, Brendan and Ronan, had died the year Liam was born. Desmond was 53 and had tried for years to have at least the one son that for a half-dozen generations had filtered down through the family of lone boys. He never saw his son Liam. He died in a car crash seven months before Liam was born. The young boy hungered all his young years for some family history to grab onto, a grasp on male ancestors all locked to their own wars.

When Liam finally came down from the attic, his grandmother said, "See anything you like? You have your pick. Anything at all."

Liam nodded. "There's an old war journal in a trunk in a corner up there. I'd like that."

"Get it now before anybody else lays a claim on it. It's yours." In his eyes she saw that he already had claimed ownership, knew he best fit it.

Liam ran up the stairs to get the journal. In the middle of the attic room he could feel someone there with him, a presence making a statement. He tried to hear the words coming out of the stillness, from the far corners and under the twin gables. He realized he was repeating some of what he had read; the words, as if spoken to him, hanging out like echoes.

And here he was now, less than a week after reading the journal, still adapting his life to a new influence; he was staring at an artist's paintings for long hours at an exhibition of the artist's Civil War work. The artist, Jeff Fiovaranti, had noticed Liam the very first day almost in a trance, eyes squinting, body taut, locked by an internal force on an external object.

From the outset, when first plagued by a vanity's reaction, Jeff sensed some other impact working on the younger man whose attention he saw was rigid, who could stare at a painting for a full half hour without moving. Jeff thought that a painter's sensitivity could best understand that reaction. It had happened to him on occasion, but he hungered for any background information, the way he searched for reasons to start a painting. In the middle of the third day of the exhibit, hundreds of people having passed through the 55 paintings only of Civil War battle sites but not battle scenes, a number of people having returned for a second viewing, he approached the mesmerized viewer.

Jeff did not know about the earlier discovery by the young man of the journal written by Ronan Craddock, born 1844, died in bed in 1925 just before his 81st birthday. For almost half a century the journal, supposedly unread by anybody in the family, had been bedded in a trunk in the corner of the old family farmhouse in New Hampshire, until such time as the family farm was going to be sold off for a huge development.

Liam, still haunted by the journal, was in turn entranced by the paintings. Jeff guessed accurately his age to be no more than 19 or 20 years, saw he had no discerning marks about him, no scars, no prominent feature, no describable sense of being other than young, healthy, interested in either the art of painting or the Civil War itself. Jeff was not sure of the latter options, but he was aware of some deep connection working on the young man. He thought it to be as strong as the many Civil War battle sites and their impact had been on him, Ground Zero acknowledgment, as Jeff called it. And he also noted that the young man kept coming back to one painting, so he thought he'd best check it out.

"Excuse me," Jeff said, "but I've noticed your interest in the exhibit for three days now, and your particular interest in this painting. My name is Jeff Fiovaranti and I know something about it. I painted it." He put out his hand.

"My name is Liam Craddock. I'm sure my great great great-grandfather fought there and his best friend was buried nearby." And Jeff listened as Liam told him the story of the journal and the impact it made on him. "It's so real to me, but especially in one place where he wrote a few words that keep ringing in the back of my head: *'Do not get separated from me ever, Ronan.'* I don't know what they mean, but they won't let go of me."

Creases on the young man's forehead inclined his thinking. He said, "Is there near that battleground a cemetery where the dead were laid to rest, Confederate dead? One that's still there, being tended?" He looked back upon the painting. "Where is this place?"

"I've been there," Jeff said, finding some of his own memories leaping to the fore. "It's the Hollywood Cemetery. There are thousands of soldiers buried there, and it's well cared for, exceptionally well. It's a large tract of land that holds some famous people. I spent a couple of days walking the grounds, noting some of the more famous names, but there are privates and generals there. He did not immediately tell Liam that he had been hit by another impact at Ronan Craddock's words, which brought back something that he heard recently; some survivors of the battleship U. S. S. Arizona, downed at Pearl Harbor in 1941, insisted they be buried with their comrades when their turn came. He felt the connection would come with awed association.

"I'm going down there," Liam said, the oath traveling with his voice. "I want to see if more of the journal hits me, if there is some action to be commissioned, if it's for me."

In a pause loaded with information Jeff could not fathom, yet was aware of, Liam Craddock continued; "I know I am being called upon. It's always been there. My grandfather said it best; 'Your turn will come, Liam, in one manner or another. You may never know the shape of its coming, but come it will, and bring you to conflict. If you never wear a uniform, you'll still be in the ranks.' I've heard that echo for years on end."

Three months later, painting a new scene of a battle site at Pickett's Mill Battlefield at Dallas, Georgia, Jeff Fiovaranti saw a local newspaper headline leap at him; YANKEE DESCENDANT DESECRATES CSA CEMETERY. It was the story of Liam Craddock, a student from Keene, New Hampshire, who had been discovered, late at night, digging up a grave at Hollywood Cemetery in Virginia. Police had been alerted by a man walking his dog late at night through the cemetery, as he was accustomed to do four or five nights a week.

Charlie Boatwright ("spell it wright, sir"), an Army veteran of the Korean War, was walking his Golden Lab, Lee Bong Ha, on one of the perimeter roads of the cemetery, when he heard what he believed to be a shovel hitting a rock. "It had that affirming sound," he said. "You'd know it from gardening, grubstaking, or digging a well. I was infuriated and thought I'd better rush the culprit, but my knees don't do me as well as they used to, so I slipped off to a neighbor's house and called the police."

"Then I went back to see what was going on, trying to get there before the police, get in a viewable position. I saw the young man, the one the police eventually arrested, working on a hole about two feet deep, handling a long-handled shovel like it was an old friend, like he knew what he was doing. Because they could not find the letter he claimed he was 'finally delivering to a comrade in arms' the authorities charged Liam Craddock with desecrating a national cemetery and eventually fined him one hundred dollars."

Most people of the area thought it a proper and fitting fine and wanted to let it go at that.

The ruse about the letter to be delivered satisfied them. It was only later the whole truth was revealed.

Charlie Boatwright, on a visit from Jeff Fiovaranti, subsequently volunteered the following information: "Before the police got there, only a few minutes as I recall, the young man in question retrieved a sort of golden pot in a somewhat ornate shape from a large bag, and with a quiet ceremony of his own, a kind of minor ritual I suspect, slipped it with care down into the hole. He placed several shovels of earth in on top of the pot. That's what he was doing when the police showed up, lights flashing all over him and the cemetery, throwing those weird shadows I'm sometimes anxious about. You never know about cemeteries, where I try to be friendly all the time because you never know who else might be visiting at the same time. The police asked what he was doing and he said he was trying to leave a letter down there for the buried person to read, but it had blown away. Most people laughed at him but to me there was quiet sincerity about the young man that perked my interest. I did not think he was a vandal. That was obvious to me, even though he was in pretty bad pickle, if I may say so. That's why I did not tell the police when they showed up that he had already put something down in the hole. They did not look for it, nor did they ask me. I was reserving judgment on the situation. It was not until later, when the police brought me down to the station, that I knew I was right, that I had done the right thing. It was then I heard the cemetery workers had filled the hole in and replaced the grass sod, which, I must tell you, was most carefully lifted out of place in the beginning. It was evident to me that there was a plan at hand, and I was in on it. Months later, young Liam wrote to me, thanking me for not giving him away, and telling me the whole story.

This is what Liam wrote to Charlie Boatwright, once a sergeant in Baker Company, 1st Battalion, 31st Infantry Regiment, 7th Infantry Division, Korea 1951-52, one of the *Polar Bears:*

Sir,

I want to thank you for what you did for me at Hollywood Cemetery that night, and how you held back some information from the police. It is appreciated very much, by me and by Sgt. Ronan Craddock, of Company C, 43rd. Georgia Infantry Regiment, Army of Tennessee. A few words in his Civil War journal really penetrated me. He wrote what his best friend and comrade Wravel Grane said to him on the morning he was to die, as if he knew it was coming: Do not get separated from me ever, Ronan.

That simple statement hung over me for a long while, but I knew what he meant, just as it came to me when I learned about sailors who survived the sinking of the USS Arizona on December 7, 1941; asking that when they finally die they be brought back aboard their ship at Pearl Harbor. Such things haunt my soul, shake it loose, and always have. In that extent I am most fortunate regardless of being in a compromising situation, seeming without reason or good excuse. Somehow I knew what that draw was, that literal magnetism, between the sergeant and his comrade. So, after much thinking and a vow that took hold of me in an instant, I got a job in a mortuary, learned a few tricks of the trade, dug up my ancestor's body and cremated him. I swear he was lost up here in Bow on the side of an overgrown hill that now holds only his sweat of years. Others in the family must have known, but it became my commission. Ronan Craddock's ashes went into the grave beside comrade Wravel Grane before the police got there, and were well-covered at their arrival. Those two soldiers are now together, as bidden, their arms at rest, peace within and without them, comrades into the face of eternity.

I trust this will put to rest any lingering doubts about your participation.

Liam Craddock, Army of the World

Salvatore Giambaressi:
Numbers Runner, Reader

The first time I saw Salvatore Giambaressi, in jeans, a Celtics windbreaker, and a Red Sox cap that could have belonged to right fielder Trot Nixon with the telltale sweat stains, he was slipping a book of poetry under his belt at the back side of well-worn dungarees. It was personal secrecy at the neighborhood level. It may seem strange and outlandish that I should be the one to tell this story, inasmuch as I was not there when it ended, and maybe it's not over yet, but be sure, the beginning fell broadly within my view. That I was tolerated in the area, the North End of Boston, came about because my mother was born there, gave birth to me there, took me when she left, brought me back later when my father died. Some thought me a displaced person, but I was tolerated, even if I was at times too curious about most things abounding in the neighborhood.

We, Salvatore and I, along with those few other people who had come in from the nasty spring rain, were drying out in a branch of the Boston Public Library, the branch at the North End's Parmenter Street. The North End's where Columbus still reigns as much as anybody, which is about all year long. Appearances said Sal had done the same secretive deed of tucking away a volume of poetry before, with no confoundment, no uncertainty in his moves. He employed a casual look about, a quick sleight of hand, and an uncompromising swift recovery from a slight hindrance when a corner of the book snagged on the windbreaker. The kid was cool.

To say the least, I was on my toes, privy to a hidden desire that ought, for obvious reasons, remain hidden.

A few moments earlier, walking behind him in the stacks, I had glimpsed the title of the slim volume, one of shy Emily's collections. The maid from Amherst had surely lured him with her words. In some unknown depth of reading and understanding, with his back to normal stack walkers, Salvatore was smiling, a wide unconscious smile. We had, I realized, similar leanings. I saw him nod a few times, eagerly, with pronouncement, as though prodding himself over one more verse or couplet, committing it to memory, to spend the day or the night with it. The touch of that diminutive lady with the far reach was on him. Without doubt, joy and swift elation flooded his face.

I found the strictly Roman face faintly brick red under his cap. A depth of intelligence filled his eyes, dark as Sicilian alleys, perhaps moody might be a better description, and a cut on his nose stated, at least to me, that he had recently been in a scrape of one sort or another, that he knew reality too. I could not see his knuckles, or the accompanying bruised remnants that might have existed there. Street survival, I surmised, knowing a bit about the terrain, the adjoining neighborhoods, and the no-nonsense lines of demarcation that city kids draw for themselves. Those lines, be it known, sometimes passed down one side of an alley, crossed the middle of a vacant lot, and leaped a broad thoroughfare, but make no mistake they were set in cement.

About this poetic young man, broad in the shoulders yet a casual litheness to him, flowed a surprising aura, one of interest, of passion and compassion, and a ready but indeterminate amount of confidence that said he could sport in more than one venue.

There was, for the moment, a host of wide contradictions; the teeming North End of Boston with its Mediterranean connection, the lonely and strange and sweet belle of Amherst, and a street kid, a poetry lover. It was a broadside of education you don't get very often. I had heard the old whispers.

Down the street or just across it, in the mild confusion of

immigrant settlements tossed everywhere around Boston, might be a numbers parlor, or a house whose occasional tenants streamed in and out at all hours of short visitations. A bakery might stand where an aged couple first baked bread and rolls, then made pizza, and then went to visit on Sundays their only son in prison.

The Celtics jacket, for one moment, caught an edge of the metered book, caused the young man a bit of a problem at his secret. About him, in a quick survey, he checked out everybody in his immediate area.

From his actions, and reactions, I was sure he was not stealing the precious volume. I just knew he was hiding it; the whole matter being that poetry, out in the streets of the North End of Boston, had few openly declared supporters, and eager lovers of poetry would suffer egregious harm once exposed. Out of all the foggy relationships I could enumerate, came the gross thought of the book being discovered in a place even young Emily had not dreamed of, and then came the view of her staunch adherent being pummeled by coarse comrades. A fifteen-year-old would ordinarily be an easy target for neighborhood toughs.

When I followed him outside, I knew he was currently employed; I saw what turned out to be his first pick-up of the day, at a small numbers parlor at the rear of a three-decker clearly slung between taller structures. Stuffing a small packet down inside a sweater inside the Celtics jacket, he sprinted down the sidewalk, crossed a busy street bearing converging streetcars, and was gone down an alley on the other side of the thoroughfare.

With graceful alacrity he moved, like a wide receiver on his appointed route. Intrigued to the absolute end, caught in the most evident ironies, I sat on a stoop in the neighborhood, watching, waiting, feeling resolution had to make itself known, knowing that this area was his neighborhood, and that he would not stray far from its confines. From a distant point on the horizon, far on the western rim of the city, I heard the shy voice from Amherst say, "My little tippler leaning against the sun."

My god, I thought, she always had a keen sense of timing.

Twenty minutes later Salvatore came out of an alley up the street about half a block on my right. Wary he was and alone, and the windbreaker, buttoned up to his neck, had added girth, which meant another bit of cargo had been added.

A quick wind with sea smells anchored in it, cursed at my ears, though it had apparently driven off the rain. April was being herself, playing games, bouncing between late winter and early summer, spring playing hide and seek. Between us were eight or ten front stoops of four-decker tenement houses, one three-decker, two small store fronts where large, smoky glass windows trapped the now-and-then streaks of sunshine at odd angles, a garage of a most suspicious nature, and a series of alleys that were street ligaments between buildings. I thought first of the bones of a skeleton connecting to the main body structure. Salvatore, on his return, closed down the distance between us, thoroughly oblivious, I thought, of my presence. My intentions, I hoped, had not been too open. Trying to convey the idea I was ignoring him, I looked over the top of my glasses, and stared at a point across the street.

That's when I first heard the voice, coming from a recess, slightly better than a whisper.

"Salvi," someone said from inside the stoop of the tenement next to me fronting on the street. Nicknames, in the North End, as in most places, carried a sense of trust in them in how they were used, and who used them. And Salvi or Sal, I assumed, were currently used in addressing my object of interest. I strained to listen. The lightness of the hidden voice, mixed with a remnant of darkness, floated out to me from the dim confine. The whisper, though soft, feminine but of some age, was clear as a Mass bell and I pictured the face of an older woman hidden away.

"Salvi," I heard again. She could have been beseeching a favor from the young runner. Or expressing a warning.

Young Giambaressi stopped in the middle of the sidewalk, as if his ears were pinned back, though he did not turn around to peer into the doorway. His arrested progress was attention enough, he could not have said any plainer, "Yes, I'm listening." He was looking across the street, away from the voice, and his raiment said he still carried some cargo of number transactions. The jacket was still puffy, and still buttoned to the neck.

"They're going to give you up for a token arrest," the older voice warned, at first in a conciliatory manner, and then it changed, instantly phlegmatic, like a hate pill had been swallowed. "That bastard, Bruno Marcante, gave it all away. You know how tight him and Mahoney the cop are, and Mahoney's captain, that Palindropo skunk."

The silky voice had gone completely granular, coming with an overtone full of understanding and warning at the same time. "He thinks you're too different. That you'll cause trouble later on. The dink fought Marco about it. Marco said he didn't care about poems, that you're faster than lightning. That's what counts. That's all that counts. But Bruno won't let go. Some of the old ones call him a *lazzarone*. And he hates your father from long ago. I don't know why. Maybe the old country. You must know the answer to that. I never knew your father in the old days." There was a pause, a sudden inhalation, and to this day I thought I heard that informant say, 'but your mother was *che bella*.' "Tell me some other time about your father, when Bruno isn't too close. He's become a real pain in the ass! He can't for a minute understand the things we like. Oh, he couldn't in a hundred year, the little snot!"

So, there was a long-time connection with them. I couldn't begin to guess what that connection was, but had to concentrate on who was hidden beyond the stoop, what personage or being, what mystery heard but not seen. I tried to picture the woman there in the recessed doorway, but none of the tenants I had noticed before fit any of the images moving on the surface of my mind, the flotation device that imagination constantly propels. The voice, in the meantime, was making full demands on my imagination. First, it brought out a kindly face, a gray-haired old woman, with a shawl discreetly in place, her chin low on a dark chest, and a ragtag, tattered ensemble of clothing capping it off; *sub rosa,* right from a Sicilian alley. She could be a hundred years old, or a hidden twenty. Disguises came and went, flitting away the way the mind plays eternal games. So awash in intrigue seemed her person that she could have been in the movies, had come right from the screen, off the stage from the Shubert or the Paramount. Then she changed, in a second coming disguised as a younger woman, svelte in the darkness, her voice silky and amorous, someone with a crush on young Giambaressi, feathers gathering in the loins, a beat of the frail heart, more real than I might have imagined.

I had to admire the runner and reader. Oh, smooth Salvatore Giambaressi! He pretended he was waving to someone across the street, perhaps up in a window of one of the tenements. "When?" he said, still staring across the street, still waving on high, the question tossed lightly over one shoulder, his eyes quickly scanning the full length of the street in both directions.

The darkened interior of the stoop answered: "It's going to be now, or today some time. Keep watch. Always know who's around. All the time, know who's around. Mahoney and Palindropo have a few weird friends. Real tattletales, scum they are. Like rats, they are, the bunch of them." The voice paused, a deep breath taken home. "They'd sell their mothers for hot tips at Suffolk Downs or Wonderland. I don't know who all of them are, but they're here, right on this street. You know every one of them." Another pause and another deep breath. "The best thing I can do for you now is to take the load from you. I will deliver it for you. They're probably up the street or around the corner right now. They're watching you. Don't be foolish and do anything that's crazy."

In the distance, thin, frail, but leveled on the air like the slap of a ruler on one's hand, came a siren's wail, as Boston, and the North End in particular, carried on its endless survival, its way of life, the street having a choreography all its own. Dust swirled and fled, cloud-borne, formless. The wind whispered renewal and the air regained a chill. For me, contrast was everywhere. From behind a small cloud, the sun leaped off windows and storefronts. Everything seemed memorial, frozen in place, yet able to be carried off in the mind, to be remembered... the sight of it, the sound of it, the smell of it, the touch of it. I was mesmerized. The wail of the siren was stiletto thin.

That frozen scene has been remembered to this moment.

And then, as though a signal had been loosed, a shot rang out, thunderous in its own way yet handgun light, a caliber quickly guessed; .22, I said to myself, pocket gun, handbag gun, a pistol a woman'd use or a tyro to the awful ranks. A window across the street was shattered. Salvatore Giambaressi dropped to his knees. I was flat on my back, clawing for cover in the doorway.

The voice in the other doorway yelled, "In here, quick, Salvi." That's when the handgun fell onto the sidewalk from somewhere above. It clattered, almost like a piece of iron pipe from a long fall. It resonated deadly echoes. Then, as an accompanying instrument, the siren's wail came closer and lost itself in other sounds. Immediately, a door slammed overhead, then another. A scream came from behind the broken window across the street, on the third floor. A few buildings down the street, three men and a woman with a big shopping bag leaped into doorways. The brakes on two automobiles jammed tight, the drivers fleeing their vehicles.

"Don't touch the gun," the hidden voice said, then filled its tone with urgency. "Get in here quick. Quick! The cops'll be here in minutes. Quick!"

Salvatore leaped into the dark doorway. Speed, it seemed assured, never left him, and he was out of sight in a second. A door slammed that sounded as though it was behind him and his ally. Another door slammed, either overhead or deeper in the building, a sucker punch of a sound. Then another door caused reverberations still deeper in the tenement. Apartments echoed. The cold-water flats gave off misgiving sounds that came hollow and mournful. Moments later a car engine kicked once, coughed a second time, and started. Then with a squeal the car sped off on the backside of the building and up a side street just as the police car pulled up in front of the building. O'Malley leaped out ahead of two other blue coats.

"Cover the back," O'Malley yelled. In his hand was a pistol, dark as death but light as a wand. He waved it at one comrade, the pistol for now his simple baton. The comrade sped down an alley. Seconds later, the way a cloud moves with a brisk wind, a sense of darkness within it, a coterie of pigeons soared off the roof of the next building, their leap into flight a wide union, and headed toward the elevated tracks. The shadow of the flight moved across the street's pavement and climbed the building opposite swift as a shot.

"They're on the roof!" O'Malley screamed. "They're on the roof!" The winged shadow had passed directly over his head, the flap of wings and the rush of air as loud as a big fan.

When Salvatore slipped into the doorway, I had slipped into the opening behind me. Garcy the crab man was coming down the stairs. "I heard a gun. You a shooter?" he said to me before he recognized me. In the dim light his glasses showed their thickness. Three times a week he pushed his two-wheeled cart loaded with cooked crabs, a nickel a piece. On the streets he would yell out a cadence; "*Squisito granchio!*" or "*Delizioso granchio!*" as if he was calling out to different people.

"If I were you, I wouldn't go out there," I said. "There's a gun in the street, and cops all over."

"They coming in here?"

"No. I think they were after Sal Giambaressi, the young runner."

"A set-up? O'Malley in it? He's a rat from way back. From the old days. Lots of people think the kid's funny because he likes poetry and nice words, but he's got balls. He ought to go to Harvard or BC sometime, somewhere on the El route. That'd be his cup of tea. Did they go next door?"

"Yes."

"Oh, shit, that's where the Nest Egg is. Even O'Malley doesn't know that." Garcy stopped dead in the middle of the stairs. It was apparent he was not getting into the mix. "I think I'll go back and get another cup of tea. Want one? C'mon."

"The Nest Egg?" I said, never having heard the expression in the neighborhood. But I went back up the stairs with him.

"Yuh, where they count and move the money. You might as well know now." He talked as he climbed back to his flat. "I haven't been in that building for over five years. I don't dare to. How come your mother came back here? Why'd you come?" He had crossed some familiar years in a matter of two steps, but he didn't wait for answers to all his questions.

The door was not locked and he let me into his flat. It was austere, neat, as though nobody lived there. There was no dust, no dirty dishes or clothes hanging about in the small kitchen. A single arrow of sunlight fell down through a window and dropped across the table. One cup, without saucer, sat on the table. A blue and red oilcloth, shiny by the one window, had a single burn mark on one edge. Two kitchen chairs with high backs sat against the table like sentinels, as though they didn't belong in the room. I caught up to a fading essence of tea on the air, then I caught a sense of something missing as I looked at an easy chair filling one corner. He fired up the stove and set the kettle atop the flame. Instantly it began to sing of steam. A calendar of the current month was pinned on the back of the door and three days each week were marked with Xs. I figured them to be his crab days.

"That was Miriam's chair," he said, noting my interest. "I guess it still is, but she's not here any more. Her and Salvi's mother were great pals. They both read to the kid all the time. There are a few punks around here who don't know a noun from a verb, not that I'd know them all. But *they* did, and Salvi does. I wish to hell he'd do something he likes with his learning, not spend his life running numbers for a few guys, them getting fancy with the money."

"Is he stuck here?"

"I can't drag him away. I talked to him. He knows what he loves, but the money comes now, the few dollars he makes. He takes care of his mother with it. That's what keeps him here. He's her son, but now he doubles as her angel." The gears shifted in his voice. "You hear that car going off out back?" He pointed out the kitchen window. "It's been there maybe for two hours, never been there before. I knew something was up, but didn't figure Salvi'd be in it."

"Somebody, a lady, maybe a girl, was hiding in the doorway and I heard her telling Salvi that O'Malley had a set-up in the works, him and Bruno Marcante. But he's such small peanuts, Salvi."

"Makes no difference to Bruno. He likes to shape people, make them his way, thinks he's an Underboss and he's only a shitpoke." The pause came, a deep breath, a secret weighed before it was spilled. "That's gotta be Donna Liberoni you heard. She's Salvi's godmother, teacher in the lower grades for a couple of years. She says Salvi's the one true student she ever had, him having this poetry thing. I don't think he grew into it. I think he's had it practically always, like a gift. Remembers everything. Knows hundreds of poems right at his tongue, so much and so quick it kind of scares me a bit. Super stuff, you know, the way it bounces. Donna found it in a hurry. She knew he was special. Probably Salvi remembers all the numbers too, the ones he carries. But I think Donna's more watchdog than teacher. And she's got a little muscle of her own, has a lot of respect out in these alleys, on these crooked little streets where breathing's tough enough as it is at any hour. But it's like Salvi's her only hope of ever getting something done, of moving on. She dreams of separation, for her choice student, being out of here, going beyond."

I'd been around the area for a while and knew a little of Donna Liberoni. "She always hang as tight as she did today, like part of his shadow? And I didn't even see her, the way she hung back in the entryway next door, a regular will o' the wisp."

"She's all the shadow she wants to be, and just for him. Dedicated she is. Maybe not fanatic, but dedicated. She doesn't hound him, but ten'll get you one she knew something was coming off today, was ready for it."

Garcy had caught my full attention. "You spin a yarn pretty good," I said.

At the kettle he said, "Always remember, you pay for a story. It takes from you. Try to find what it gives back, if it ever does."

They had me again, Garcy the crabman, along with Salvi the numbers runner and poetry lover. I could see my mother nodding at me, smiling, as I sat in the corner of a distant winter kitchen, reading a book, absorbed, oblivious to all but her and the words spinning in front of me.

We had separated from the noises, from Salvi and Donna Liberoni, from O'Malley the cop, and were ever distant from the Nest Egg. But there came, as if from a deep canyon, from the guts of the building next door with a four foot alley between structures, loud banging, harsh demands mostly inarticulate in their threats. Then a gunshot was heard.

I heard O'Malley finally scream out, "Where's that goddamn kid? I want him now!"

Another voice, at the backside of the building, yelled out, "He ain't here, O'Malley. He's gone!" A door slammed or was rammed. Even our building shook.

"A voice yelled out, "If I was you, O'Malley, I wouldn't go in there."

Garcy the crabman touched me on the arm. "Oh, Jeezus, O'Malley's at the Nest Egg." With a slight nod, a sparkle in his eyes, he said, "He just got himself screwed. It looks like a blind move to get in that room. He can take every dime he finds, but it won't pay off in the long run. You can bet on that."

That's the way it went, of course. O'Malley toted off a box of money as evidence. It was said, bantered around the streets free as you like, that less than a third of it ended up at the police station. Salvi's name was associated with the gun found in the street, O'Malley saying he most likely had fired it, that there wasn't all that much money taken from the numbers room he had busted into, that Salvi was their only runner.

When Donna Liberoni stepped up and made her statement, O'Malley backed down, knowing what the odds were. The whole North End knew what her sole interest was, the kid who loved poetry, Salvi the numbers runner. So, ultimately, in spite of O'Malley's first dictate, Salvi was not charged with anything, but he did stop running numbers. His patron saint had finally gotten into his soul, pointing out what was coming down the road to him, showing him how crooked even the beat cop was, insisting there were poems not yet written that someone had to write

My report, though far from the finish, has come a long way now. Donna Liberoni, with persistence, got him into St. John's Prep School well north of the North End. He was boarded in a private home in Danvers, became a stick-out wide receiver for their football team, graduated from Boston College out at the end of the Green Line. In his time there he gave up the football, found a few more words he had not seen together before, heard the voice working inside his head, wrote poems that still make Donna Liberoni cry with happiness.

Once in a while I bump into Garcy the crabman. He tells me that Salvi's mother is still living in her old place, and that Salvi visits often. We talk about that day when things changed for Salvi, see some of his poems in magazines, and each of us holding dear his own copy of Salvi's first book of poems, *Donna's Last Word on the Street.*

Shag Debrillen, Brickie

(or The Usual Flat-out Failure at Most Things Unexceptional)

A s Shag DeBrillen was about to turn the corner in the suburban area where he lived, he spotted a lone car a short ways down the town road. He whistled and told himself it was an Impala, an oldie, an olden golden, a gem of an antique. With the six ports in the rear end looking like gun ports on a fighter aircraft, he affirmed it was a '63. The car was parked at a siding and the driver, leaning out the window, was talking to a young girl of ten or so that Shag assumed was on her way to school.

He wondered if he was looking at an illusion of sorts, not thinking he was really seeing what he was seeing; there was too much nothing around the scene. An old car, a young girl, not much else to look at, or take your eye to the quick. Sometimes what you see is not what you see.

It was early October and school year had recently started. Soon, he thought, the leaves would begin to change color, the big silver maple directly across from him soaking up the early sunlight, the threat of change poised and real in its broad cast of leaves. The nights would come cooler in a matter of a week or so, the year looking at its cold ending.

The front of his old Pontiac, a '76 Bonneville, with the Indian head yet proudly mounted by his own hand on the hood, nosed out into the cross road. Shag DeBrillen knew another *minor* accident would probably finish off the car. He'd had enough of them, he recalled quickly, a few snickers mixed in with the recollections. So the car was driven gingerly, as Stockwell his plumber buddy had noted: "Hey, man, ole Shag drives the bucket like it was Aunt Mindy's sewing machine, I swear to God."

Shag had a piece of sheet metal and an old wire coat hanger wrapped around the muffler. Each day he'd tighten up the coat hanger or add a new one, wary of the cops who had warned him about excess noise, Trupote being the nastiest about it, a smartass rookie to begin with. Tenuous at best, a front-end rocker arm sent tremors that were known in his hands and arms at each turn on the road. The amount of oil usually burning now in the old engine, he surmised hurriedly on numerous occasions, would float a rowboat. Besides, the exhaust smell was real and dark. *Unreliable* was the word consciously coming into his vocabulary, working its way in on a daily basis. At 168,000 miles the old sedan was counting the miles as well as the days. It was just about good enough to get him to the next wall he was working on. One more solid day's work in the offing; another brick, another tier, another wall.

Suddenly, up there ahead of him, a hand snaked out of the Impala and snatched the young girl, perhaps ten years old he said again to himself, into the car.

Shag sat straighter in his seat, quickly upright, and his foot locked onto the brake pedal. Blond tresses, bleached from constant sun, fell over his forehead the hot summer had painted a dark tan. He felt as inert as a concrete block. Something almost physical caught in his throat, caught and grabbed on harsh as fishing barbs. For a fraction of a moment he thought he would choke. Mary Gibbons, now mysteriously gone these many years, leaped into his mind. Once more he saw her pretty face ringed with dark curls in the seat right beside him in the Mrs. Stone's third grade class. She'd been pretty as a picture. Once her slip had shown as white as snow. That glimpse was more than half his lifetime earlier. A breathtaking dizziness flooded his head and his hands froze on the wheel. From that last day going home from school, not a soul had seen pretty Mary Gibbons. Twenty years of nothing.

The Impala, in a surging motion, took off down the town road, dust lifting behind it in a minor contrail. The rear ports, like a logo or a full name across the back of the vehicle, kept saying *Chevy.*

Shag DeBrillen earlier in age had blown about all his schooling and then his one attempt at a G.E.D. Plain and simple it came up for him, books and numbers had little place in his life. He was a brickie; of *that* he was absolutely positive. His hands told him where he belonged. That perfect line necessary on a wall was scored into his eyes. It had been there since the day Marsellaise, the old neighborhood mason, had shown him eighty years' worth of tricks of the trade.

"Illusion is important to a mason," Marsellaise had said. "Make it work for you. Then do your thing." Shag took that release all the way, figuring he already had a head start on things; he had worn his hair the way he wanted to, ever since his father had beaten him for not wearing it the way "grown and proud men do."

Shag knew brick laying and cars and little else.

Now decisions came abruptly at him, the kind he felt he was not capable of making. In a kind of desperation, he began to talk to himself. At least the sound was there: *There's no illusion here. No second sighting down the line of a wall, no chance to reset a stone or brick in an otherwise perfect wall. Can't use a piece of string for this.*

The gas pedal kicked at his tromped foot. *Perhaps I can get the number on the registration plate. It's all I can hope to do; there'd be no way this old junk can catch that other car.* The engine coughed and kicked and sounded just like old Marsellaise the day he died at the end of a long wall, a day's work done, a lifetime of work done. It had been ten minutes before the workday was supposed to be over when the old gent kicked over, true to the bitter end.

In the rearview mirror he saw the plume of black exhaust flowing out behind him. Momentarily he smelled the exhaust, and then discounted it. The picture of the girl's mother came to him, cleaning the kitchen from the breakfast meal, probably a yellow apron about her waist like his mother used to wear, yellow as the morning sun in the early slant or a whistling canary, planning lunch or the evening meal, pleasant time on hand. *Oh, damn, this can be the worst of days for her and she has no idea yet. No idea!*

The engine snorted and kicked back again at his pedal foot. The smell of oil was heavier, the wake of exhaust as wide as the road behind him. In the back seat his trowels rattled against one another and one clinked against the hammer's head, sounding out the single tick of a clock. An empty plastic bucket fell off the seat. *If there's a car behind me, I can't see it. Maybe a cop's back there. I damn sure wish a cop was there. I need a cop. I need a cop. What the hell can I do in this claptrap! Goddamn it!*

He stepped on the gas again. The car shook again. Down the road ahead of him the Impala was pulling away. A half mile down the road a yellow Bluebird school bus had a side red octagonal flag flung out at its pick-up stop. Two or three cars were stopped coming from the other direction. One was a pick-up truck. *I wonder if it could be Stockwell on his way to work. I hope so. That Dodge of his can do a hundred if he wanted it to.* The abductor's Impala slowed and stopped and Shag crept up behind it and got the number on the plate. *781-Q77. That's easy,* he said to himself. He wrote the number boldly on his arm with his stubby work pencil. The figures were scrawling and uneven but fully legible. On a second thought he wrote the number on his jeans. The pencil felt as though it was cutting into the skin of his thigh.

Shag spoke aloud, "I should get out of the car and approach the other car, rip open the door, get the guy out before he could take off. But the guy will see me and take off. I'll lose time. I've got to be smart about this. Here I am, a goddamn brickie. What the hell can I do? I need a cop. Ain't that a laugh." He could hear the echo of his voice, helpless and languid, distant as a star. Once when he was sick he had felt like this. Never had he begged for anything, not when sick, not even for his G.E.D. *I need a cop. I need a cop.* He looked behind him, back down the road, the exhaust fumes momentarily thinned out and the air clearer. Nothing was in sight behind him. Nothing as far back as he could see.

The red arm on the bus folded and a Buick came past the bus from the other way. The Impala snaked slowly out over the double line and dipped back as the pick-up came abreast of the bus. It was not Stockwell's truck, but it was a speedy new Dodge Ram 2500. It came beside Shag. Its engine roared and then flew past him. In front, the Impala slipped around the bus and headed down the road. Shag could not see the girl moving in the car. "Oh, damn," he said. The sound of his voice was fainter, receding with his hope.

Marsellaise's voice came in a rugged whisper. *Illusion*, it said. *Illusion*. That old man was still trying to teach him something, Marsellaise being noisy again.

The police car came out of a side road and headed toward him. Marsellaise was still talking to him, now noisy and incoherently it seemed, a mesh of gibberish and accent from an old man long gone. The white and blue said it was a state police cruiser, one man behind the wheel. Shag shook his head, trying to shake off the voice, the sense of illusion still at him, the loudness. He was trying to concentrate on something. It was difficult, the damn voice of the old mason refusing to let go. *Pretense, Illusion*, it kept saying. What was Marsellaise at? Where was his voice coming from? This blue and white car was real, wasn't it? Shag leaned over the wheel, faked inertness, lack of attention, yet kept the Bonneville straddling the double traffic lines. The shadow of the cruiser slipped beside him with a roar. The squeal of brakes came from behind. Shag leaned on the gas pedal. The old bucket had some life in it yet, something beside the guttural grunts. But not enough. Moments later the cruiser roared up behind him.

Ahead, the Impala was moving off as small as the head of a pencil.

Shag came to an abrupt stop. He leaped from the Bonneville as the trooper came out of the cruiser directly behind him. Shag waved his arms, tried to scream, his blond curls shaking all over, the tanned face red with excitement. The eyes were popping in his face like glazed saucers. Desperate breath rushed into and filled his throat. Words tried to claw their way through, almost scratching his throat. He looked like an actor in serious trouble, on stage, forgetting his lines, the audience on the edge of their seats. Then he pointed up the road, out of town. "That Impala, plate number *781-Q77.* The driver grabbed a little girl back there."

God, he was coherent!

The trooper smiled and said, "This your car? You Shag DeBrillen? You old Trupote's favorite driver in these parts? I haven't seen one of these things since my Uncle Henry was around." His hand was on the fender of the Bonneville. "Man, I heard all about you. Tru says he can hear you coming before he sees you. That a fact?"

"Listen, that '63 Impala driver grabbed a little girl back there about a mile. Yanked her right into the car. You gotta do something about it."

"I don't gotta do anything about nothing! Old Trupote said you had a hundred stories. This another one? A new one?" The trooper cocked his head, noting that he was tuning in the loud muffler. A smile crossed his face.

Shag heard Marsellaise's voice coming from behind his car. *Illusion,* it said. *Illusion. Lie,* it also said. *Lie like hell or force the issue.*

"It's gonna be your ass, not mine, when I tell this story."

"Don't threaten me! You got a rep, that's for sure. I heard about the time the pawn shop was ripped off and you gave the locals a plate number because you saw something. Cops chased an old teacher of yours almost to the New York border. Scared the damn hell out of her and she said you were paying her back for something she'd done to you years ago."

Shag came back quickly. "That was an old maid busybody who manufactured that. I gave a number and the dispatcher screwed it up. In this case, it's the little girl who's threatened." He pointed down the road out of town. "A couple of more miles, out of the lake region, and they'll get away. That's when your ass will be in a wringer."

The trooper smiled. "I don't take to threats. Trupote said you had a talent for this stuff. Could lie like a trooper." He smiled at his own words. "Play the game for all it's worth."

"Well, think about her mother sitting home and you're sitting here shaking your dick at the side of the road 'cause you caught a guy with a loud muffler and her little girl is grabbed by some guy and making it out of town right about now." He again pointed out of town, the small pencil dot of an Impala barely visible at a big curve in the road as it began a sweep around Lake Chagmond.

With no expression on the trooper's face, Marsellaise's voice came back. *Lie like hell*, it said. *Lie like hell because she's worth it, that little girl. And her mother putting around the kitchen right about now, dumb as she'll ever get.*

The old vision came back. Marsellaise was scribing a line with a string, pegging it. At one point he put stress on the string, "Right about here. Here's where you do a little double dip, an eye catcher. This grabs their eye, right here. You know you can't make a wall that looks straight without them saying their piece about it. Here's where you lie like hell." He had snapped the string.

Shag was thinking of Marsellaise's words, "Make a good excuse for this and you're home free with the whole thing." So Shag said, "What's your name, officer?" He put a smirk on his face.

"You want my badge number too, wise guy? 6-7-2, and remember it." His rancor was still riding the air when Marsellaise took the opportunity to come back. The trooper put his thumb behind the badge and nearly popped it into Shag's face. "*6-7-2!*" The smirk was returned wholesale with the gesture. "I think you'll find out sooner than later, my friend, that when you're talking to the police you better drop the wise-ass stuff. It'll do you better in the long run."

The car, said Marsellaise. *The car. The car.* Then it came heavy. *The cruiser. Damn it, Shag, the cruiser.* Then he punctuated his words. *Illusion*, he said, his voice suddenly softer, testing him, cajoling. *It's our only chance!*

To Shag, the *our* was all inclusive. It meant the little girl, her mother and father, perhaps siblings, *6-7-2* with the smirk still on his face, Marsellaise, and of course, the pariah, the loser, Shag himself caught up again. Life will never change, he thought. I might have thought I've been shortchanged forever, but now's not the time. A tree caught in the morning sun almost blazed up on the side of the road as the sun smashed into it. Summer was gone. Fall was here. Winter was coming. Loneliness, terror of the worst sort, could be coming to a mother behind him, toward the center of town.

Down the road Shag looked, out of town. And the telltale dot of the Impala was gone. Panic reared its ugly head, and then backed off as he tried to visualize the map of the area. What side roads there were. What was the nearest intersection for the Impala to find flight? Who patrolled out there if it wasn't this obnoxious son of a bitch? The whole string of summer cottages along the one side of the lake snaked into his mind. They'd all be shut up now, the summer traipsed away and gone, nobody around.

Time was running as fast as the Impala. Shag felt the *now-or-never* crunch pounding down on top of him. It was worth it all, even what he could see coming at him, as clear as he could ever see anything, and the mother in her apron, in her kitchen, oblivious to all of it. He tried to keep the little girl's fate out of his mind. Tried not to see her in some helpless position, some animal of a man hovering over her. The shock went through his body, snapped into the back of his head, he swore he could hear Mary Gibbon's laughter, see her face once more, the brown hair, the red lips, the big eyes. Perhaps he heard her cry out, an endless plaintive cry that would last forever. He shivered and caught himself at the edge of something new. Marsellaise was as near as ever, that good old son of a bitch brickie not letting go, not leaving him.

Coyly, Shag said, "I thought you were getting a flat tire when I saw you coming," thinking, If he's as stupid as he looks, I'll have a chance.

6-7-2 looked at the street side of his cruiser, bending over, being sure. One hand touched the rear tire as though he didn't believe his own eyes. The other hand was on his holster, as if he were still in class at the academy and being put to a test. The tire was okay. He walked to the back of the car and bent to look at the other rear tire.

That's when Shag heard Marsellaise as if he were standing just behind him, sharing the same shadow.

Now! the single word was like a roar.

It hit Shag between the eyes like a baseball bat in the hands of the Red Sox rightfielder Trot Nixon or the big guy David *Papi* Ortiz, world champs, the two of them.

Now!

Swearing the whole world could hear the long-dead mason, he leaped at the car, praying not to stumble, not to screw up again, not to fail miserably at perhaps the only good thing he might ever do in his whole life. Pulling the door open, he jumped into the cruiser, snapped the door lock down and jammed the engine into *Drive*.

The gears ground harsh as an old cement mixer, then caught, meshed, brought a sudden speed to the take-off. With a roar the cruiser leaped off the shoulder, spent rubber, leaving smoke, and rocketed down the road. *6-7-2* leaped, cursed, and went for his gun. From behind him and from the other direction, cars were coming. He holstered his weapon. The portable radio came off his hip. He yelled into it.

Other than being a brickie, Shag knew he could drive. He'd been driving, whether anyone liked it or not, since he was eleven, more than once at the wheel of a "borrowed" car: his father's, his Uncle Harry's, Bert Wills' who lived next door and always left the keys in the car after a night on the town. Good old Bert never missed the car on a dozen occasions. The last ride was the best, the cops chasing Shag over half the town, and he slipped out of Bert's car and into the house without anybody the wiser. Ten minutes later he saw Bert, shaking his head, yelling, being hauled off by the cops. Shag had laughed himself to sleep.

The cruiser was now doing about eighty miles an hour as Shag began the loop about the lake. The lake surface, off to his left, through trees, cottages, cabanas, was a silver blue, catching a piece of the morning sky in it. Yet it was a cool blue, making his fingers feel icy. Another shiver came to him as he thought of the coming winter on an open staging, the unset bricks piled at hand on the staging, the wind blowing out of the northeast, some arrogant son of a bitch of a boss yelling up from a heated truck cab down below. The sun poked fingers through decorative camp trees, in gaps between the cottages and cabanas, and spread itself in the maple treetops off to his right, color catching as if being crayoned in at the same moment.

In the straightaway, as the curve about the lake was left behind, there appeared no pencil-dotted Impala ahead of him. Christ, he could be gone forever, and the kid with him. Shag tromped on the accelerator and felt his back punch against the seat. He'd get this son of a bitch car up to a hundred if he could. If the Impala got to the turnpike they'd have a cold shot in hell of finding it, and the kid with it.

Even then the old mason wasn't letting go. Shag heard *Illusion* again, Marsellaise's voice coming as if from the back seat, another unauthorized passenger.

The radio popped alive. "Unauthorized driver at the wheel of a stolen state police car, westbound out of Saxon on the lake road. Driver is dangerous. Post blockade short of the turnpike exit. Trooper afoot at the Hanscombe Road intersection. Needs assistance."

Hell, they'd be on him in minutes, the Impala probably going right on by them, the little girl maybe knocked unconscious in the back seat. He tromped harder on the accelerator.

And then, his heart near pounding in his chest, pressure building in his head, his hand now sweaty instead of cold, he caught sight of a glare of light between two small and obviously empty cabins on the edge of the lake. It was like a barrel of a rifle from a distant point and John Wayne or James Arness picking it out of a vast expanse of otherwise darkness. It was the six rear ports of the Impala, all six of them blinking at him at the same time. He was dead sure about it, and the vehicle was parked between the two small buildings, and partly under a small clutch of trees.

Shag braked down, went by the two cabins less than a hundred feet off the road. Don't squeal the brakes, he told himself. Easy does it. Leave the cruiser here in the middle of the road. If *6-7-2* has made contact, someone'll be here soon enough.

He climbed out of the cruiser, after setting the emergency brake, leaving the keys in the ignition switch, the engine running.

Behind a clutch of brush and small trees, he picked up a half dozen stones and made an arrow in front of the cruiser, pointing back to the Impala. Doubt hit him. He knew it was a cover-your-ass gesture. It made him sick about himself. He slipped down into the brush. His heart came pounding again, his hands cold in return, then hot in a hurry.

He neared the Impala. Silence sat on the lake, now bluer and brighter, and in the air. There were no cries. No strange sounds. No struggle evident to his senses, but an overwhelming strangeness crowding him. He was feeling hatred for something part human, an ogre, a monster, a child-thief. Bile suddenly loaded his throat with a sour burning. His hand closed on a rock of good size. His huge brickie hand closed down on it as if it were a baseball in the hand of Curt Schilling or Pedro Martinez. Two fingers curled tightly about the rock. He had to stop whatever was in process right now. Get him out in the open. He'd take his chances with him, the driver, the abductor, that rotten son of a bitch. The unknowing mother in her yellow apron in her quiet kitchen came back to him. The helpless girl leaped into his mind, her hands reaching for her mother. For her father. For him. The bile loaded itself again. He gagged and recovered. In one swift move, standing upright about thirty feet from the nearest cabin, he fired the rock at the single window facing him. He missed the window by a foot, but the rock rattled loud as a gunshot against the side of the cabin. Sounds came to him from the interior of the cabin. A sudden noise of banging objects. The scream of a little girl. The sounds of quick bedlam. Back over his shoulder he heard sirens screaming across the lake as if a police speedboat were approaching. They were coming from the turnpike end of the road, he was sure, all out to help a brother officer.

Then, as Shag turned back, a single male, tall, moving quickly, made his way out of the cabin. He limped. He had a beard. His jacket was blue and worn. Even with the limp he moved rapidly, perhaps desperately. There was another scream from inside. Shag's heart pounded as the man raced to the Impala.

Shag threw another rock. This one smashed against the rear window of the Impala and shattered it. The man heard the sirens. Seeing Shag, he jumped into the car and the car shook as the ignition caught in a roar. Sand and debris rose by the rear wheels as he backed the car. Shag hurled another rock, smashing against the side of the Impala. The engine died, coughed, started again. The sirens were closer. The car coughed and gagged and coughed anew. Then the engine caught again. The Impala swung toward the road as two police cruisers, one a state vehicle, the other a town police car, came to a stop beside the cruiser stranded in the middle of the road. Two uniforms leaped out.

Shag screamed, "Stop him. He's the one who grabbed the girl. She's in the cabin." He raced to the cabin as the two more police cars converged on the Impala caught on an embankment on its underside, the wheels spinning harmlessly, the old engine letting go its final cries.

Shag DeBrillen, quicker than he'd ever been, ran to the cabin and found the girl crouched on an unmade bed. She screamed once more, shook all over, and then her mouth and lips were caught in a sudden silence. He held his huge and ungainly hand out, and said, easily, softly, all the kindness in his voice he could muster. "Your mother sent me."

Outside there was as single shot. A voice screamed, "Halt."

"They got him," Shag said. "They got him."

The brickie put his arms tenderly around the little girl, and her arms came around him. She had dark hair and big eyes. Tears flowed from her eyes. Could be that in the classroom a boy next to her stole quick glances at her all the time.

Shag thought all that was coming to him would be worth all of this, this one sweetness in his whole life. He could picture the girl's mother, in her canary yellow apron, in her quiet kitchen, looking out the window, admiring the leaves that were changing colors, winter down the road a ways yet. As far as she was concerned, this far in the new day, nothing but winter was coming her way, nothing out of the ordinary.

The Gang from the Boatyard

The gang from the boatyard, by God you had to love 'em, the lot of them, every man jack of them: braised, poured, scratched, abraded, welded, mucked about by all of life, you had to love 'em. Up front you have to know that those who had gotten nicknames felt honored, for that moniker stuff usually came from within, a private medal of sorts, earned without hoopla, seared forever. Those who hadn't been so acclaimed patiently waited some kind of anointment, slow in coming, taking over like a root, underneath everything seen or known. Some of them had names like Max, Slad, Wilf, Muckles, Shag, RonnieJ, Slip, a feast of designations varied as character. And the sole captain of his own boat in the lot of them was Shanklin Garuf.

To a man, you had to love 'em.

Outside of Shanklin Garuf who had the gift of property, but who stood by his buddies in all kinds of weather, they were interchangeable elements; reliable, quiet, worn in many of their parts by life, to a man. Dip Connors, friend and local detective, said any one of them looking in a mirror might see the form of any other of that crew. Dip said they were, in spite of shadows worn like vague amulets, the most real people in town. Light, he believed, sat in their eyes, a detention, an absorption only distance or knowledge allows. A compression of the ages, a mute exchange of information, like the bonding the Cro-Magnons had no word for. None of them, outside of a congruent celebratory boisterousness now and then, had ever given the citizenry of Saugus any due cause for alarm. They labored much of life. They fought a war or two, hurt a foe or two. They tired. They came on age. They were stars and stripes guys without the parade, a kind of phalanx of maturity in dungarees or corduroys, Bruins or Celtics or Patriots windbreakers, ball caps with championship logos from Saugus Little League or Saugus High hockey proudly worn. They ate apple pie with their coffee, drove Chevie or Ford pick-up trucks into or out of the lobster boat landing or the boatyard, and moved as a body into their second millennium.

And then there was murder.

Max Cargo came upon Shanklin Garuf spread-eagled on the dock and right beside his boat. It was just before 5 a.m. A ball of breath grabbed Max where it hurt the most, in the righteous neighborhood, right next door to his heart, a ball peen in a short swing. Old Shanklin was a real pal and Max's breath caught again, the old quad by-pass never far away, a scar if there ever was one. The thought leaped through him, *Not now! Not two of us and morning still coming on.* At length he breathed deeply, clearly.

The sun, still hidden behind Pine Hill in Lynn across the river from the boatyard, seemed to threaten appearance. A sudden fear hit him that Pine Hill had captured the sun, or would detain it. Salt smell rose up from the Saugus River and a breath of April air touched at Max's face with early tenderness, cool alert. Contrast overwhelmed him. One look at the prone man and Max knew he had been knocked asunder and then some. Kneeling sorely and gingerly, knowing his arm strength was still enormous though his knees had deserted him with cause, the swung peen known still in his chest harsh as a strident echo, he touched the captain. His fingers went electric, a shock of knowledge passing up through them. There was no rise to Shanklin's chest. No apparent breath. No detection at the wrist. The night before the captain had asked for one man's help for the morning and Max had said he'd do it. Max was an early riser but now he had this; Shanklin, *and somebody else*, had arrived at the dock ahead of him.

Max called the cops, telling them all he had done was close the captain's eyes, put his ball cap over them. Besides calling them it was the least he could do, being a momentary salutation in its own right. Contrasts still eating him, he felt irritated at the pretty morning as it came down on him, coming with a lazy stretch out of the eastern marsh with flooding sunlight. The early chirping and signature of birds and the shadowing hover of thermal-lifted gulls bothered him, the hushing touch of swells coasting upriver and washing in against the pier supports seemed wasteful energy; morning coming odd without an old pal.

Contiguously, with clarity, with a specter of pictures, he remembered how haunting the loss of Ace Burleson was the night Ace just fell off the dock, how there was only a splash and nothing ever after to fill up Ace's space. Then, with more pictures crying for company, as if summoned from the semi-darkness, came an oblique tenderness he thought might not have come his way before. Calvin Boone rose up, a black comrade in the 31st Regiment in Korea, and that association fifty years old, that kinship, blistered him with recollection: Calvin, a dark giant of a man, a unique softness, just ahead of him on the hill, stiffening, dropping, reaching one hand to touch someone, something. Calvin's hand had found Max's hand. Then that winged obliqueness hit Max frontally and found doors to all parts of his body, doors opened for the first time in years. To his feet it plummeted like a bird out of the sky, locking him up with the most excruciating tenderness he had ever known. The pictures faded immediately; Calvin went away, Ace went away, Shanklin went away, but the unmitigated tenderness found a lost home and stayed with him a long while. Even later interrogation could not dislodge its wings.

Max knew how the gang would feel, what they would know. After all, they were brothers at the core. From all he had interpreted, *this* is what he first understood.

Before noon was at hand Detective Dip Connors talked to the lot of them, counted all of them as mere background to the crime, and began his investigation. Their poker game, near forty years old and still moving on, had kept eight of the gang on the second floor of the yacht club for most of the previous night. Looking at the roster Dip knew of six knee replacements, three quad bypasses, one hint of melanoma, and two *kinda-touching-the-game* cases of arthritis. There was not a rock-lifter in the bunch. For something heavy had slammed Captain Shanklin Garuf on the top of his skull, an object such as a rock with a solid, roundhouse, over-the-head kind of swing. Dip had assured himself it was not the swing of a card player, not a poker player.

"You saw nothing. You heard nothing. You remember nothing out of the usual with Cap and any acquaintance. No arguments or ill will. Have I got that all straight?" Dip had them all on the first floor of the yacht club, at the small bar. They stared at him the whole time he was talking, knowing he was at his work no matter where it took him. His eyes were bright, his gaze firm, his mouth moving with a slow deliberate measure. A shine sat on his cheeks and forehead, as if the tie he wore was knotted out of place. For a dozen years he had been out of the uniform phase and into detective work. They knew he was a plodder. A draft horse. Slow but relentless. "I am going to need help on this. I am counting you all out of this and all in it with me, right up to our necks." The pause was electric. "I know he was one of you. That counts with me. It always has. I know each one of you like I know my own brothers. That counts." Dip knew he could have written a biography of each one, beginning with a deck of cards and discrete copies of DD-214 service separations.

Some of the yard dogs played 45, some Hearts, some Cribbage. The games were important to them, filled their days and nights when at them, and with talk about them when away from the tables. The games were in the back room of the yacht club, on the first floor, a most modest building scratched against the riverbank. Most of the money of the yacht club, for it was a meager place to begin with, more a clubhouse than a boathouse, was on the poker table and that had to have its own protection from noise and other

surprises, therefore its home was on the second floor, back end.
Wilf Gamin was the only non-card player in the lot of the gamey
crew. Odd, loose times for him were spent scribbling in a journal.
"My mother always told me to keep a record of my life." He had
sixty-two notebooks of that life. None of his pals had read a single
page. No one pushed him for show.

A few days later Dip was talking to the chief. "Their hard lot is
their history, not in any current malevolence. They're not thieves
or murderers. They're old laborers, they're card players, they knock
down nothing more than a few stiff drinks once in a while. To a
man they've paid their dues of one sort or another. Seen a kind of
hell that they've put behind them, until this." He pointed at the
crime folder on his desk. It said *Shanklin Garuth, Boat Captain.*
It also said *Murder* in capital letters. "That lot of men all served in
one war or another, except Slip who was never able to do anything
like that with his bad arm. Had a couple of POWs in the crowd,
Europe and Korea, couple of Bronze Stars, a Silver Star too, I bet
a half dozen Purple Hearts, but no story tellers. They wear their
travels well as they can. The kind of guys I'd want beside me in
hell or down an alley come a troubling night."

"You think this was for robbery?" said the chief. "Somebody
caught in the act? Somebody hit the captain with a board or a
spike or a chunk of iron? No report of anything missing, if there
was anything there on the boat in the first place. What about
revenge for some old cause? What about relatives in the mix?"

"That'd be pure guess work, coming up on that," Dip said.
"Cap plugged along in life before and after an old aunt left him
some dough to buy the boat, and that was damn good number of
years ago. I think in '76. Don't know any harsh words ever spoken
about him. None he said himself. They swear that to a man. Trouble
is some of them don't have a hell of a lot of keen memory any
more, hazy being what might describe it. And some of them will
be gone before this gets closed for good." He filed the folder in a
desk drawer, the move and the thought of mortality being
punctuation at its best.

"Well, we'll see what comes out of the relative angle, what else touches on the edges."

The chief patted Dip on the back, then said, "I know I've been here a lot less than you, and I can't always agree with you, but someone would think you think the sun rises and sets on a bunch of boatyard turkeys. They are not the end of the world, Dip. They are not hero class in the purest sense. I don't know how all this wraps up in you. You and them." He nodded at wherever in the outside world, but was signifying the boatyard and the quintessential gang without a doubt.

"Come time, chief," Dip said, "and you'll know the difference."

It was a month later, Phil's Nearby Restaurant was dim, Tommy's Plastic Shop shuttered, the boatyard and docks quiet, the yacht club downstairs empty late at night, the crew of them in the back room upstairs. Not at poker but at talk.

Sledge Crafton, noted for his strength and mostly inertia of the mouth, his eyes deeper than normal, said, "Old Dip's been through us and marked us clean, but he's that known bloodhound he swore he'd be. If he keeps getting stumped he'll be back. Appears like he's got nowhere yet and nowhere to go, so he'll go over the whole track." He nodded his head and added, "Time and again. Time and again." To a man it was acceptable bitching.

"Christ, Sledge," advised Slad Glasko, "he knows none of us had a hand in Cap's death. What's he coming back for if we ain't got nothing for him?"

"Way he works, Slad, knocking things together. We saw that when old Henry was robbed and knocked around a year or so ago. He got to those wise-ass kids because he wouldn't let go. So we know he's going to be around. It started here and will probably end here, whatever the route takes him. What we got to do, and why we said we'd come here, is to do the same thing ourselves. Hell, we owe it to Cap to do anything we can, what he's done for us over the years. All I know is I know nothing but I'm here. If it's only to shake something out of the damn trees, I'm for it. We're all for it. Does anybody know more than the nothing I know? Sheet, I feel so damn ignorant it hurts my balls."

Long into the night they talked and never came past their ignorance of the whole situation, and especially the night in particular, all at their games and then all at their sleep. None of them, except Max, ever scratched at daylight without an effort for a good number of years, Max the morning insomniac.

"Cap could get most things from me," said Tyledge Bracknus, "except the goodness from my laying in in the morning. Couldn't a got me out of the sack with dynamite that day, way we played that night." He looked at Slip, remembered the look on his face that night and offered, "You gotta remember that last draw, Slip. I been thinking about luck ever since, way they came up for you the last hand out, was all of 2 a.m. by then. That was shit luck, man, shit luck of the highest order. You must be paying for it yet outta the winnings."

Slip nodded his agreement and said, "Lady Luck with the cards always takes a turn where you might never expect her, so you don't brag on her or ask her to dance with you more than you ought. More often than not it's Ladies' Choice." For the sprinkling of smiles he nodded in self-agreement, an adage coined in the boatyard.

They talked for hours. Nothing clear, open, or previously undisclosed came out of their communal efforts. Dawn was threatening. They split and went to their sleep. Some of them into dreams as quick as a snore. Some rumbled thinking about Cap being slipped in from behind by an unknown person, the hand swinging hard, the crunch on the head. Nothing came from memory or dream.

And so it was with Dip Connors, two additional months parked on top of the case, as if it is to be buried as deep as Captain Shanklin Garuth. At the station he tells the chief he is buried with nothing all atop him, him and his case. "There's no clue, no recognition, no witness, absolutely nothing to even get hold of. Buried under nothing. It's all so clean, so damn clean. There has got to be the first piece of the puzzle just lying around waiting to get picked up by thumb and forefinger. Snapped up. I know it." His eyes narrow their sudden intensity. "Guess I'll go back again. Them boys be mad as hell seeing me come back so soon, nothing in my hand."

Dip entered the boat yard from the parking lot. He stepped onto the small dock again, the evening sun bouncing off the small swells of the river, the clear smell of the ocean alive on the river. He swore he could hear Shanklin Garuth trying to talk to him.

Muckles Brown, looking out the window onto the river, said, "Dip's back, boys. He's coming in again." They turned as Dip slipped in the side door like a man hunting deer, soft shoed, quiet, not looking to startle anybody.

He was thinking to himself, as he looked at them looking at him: *I know each one like I know my brothers. I'd trust each one like I'd trust my brothers. Is there anything I never knew about my brothers? Anything unknown about these guys who I really like?* There was nothing unknown. At least of a value in this case. It was only when he looked at Wilfred Gamin that he knew at least one thing was unknown, how Wilf had looked at life in the pages of his journals. *What secrets were there? What secrets could be shared? What small tidbit might come alive from his years of observation?* He had to try, he vowed. *There's nothing else.*

Again, as it had before, the thought came that he could write a biography for each one of them. Obviously at the moment Wilf Gamin was the prime object of a ready portrayal, and Dip could remember drawing him easily and carefully out of a car wreck a good dozen years earlier, both ears torn, his jaw broken, part of his scalp peeled back as if a skilled tomahawk had done its work. Wilf's words came back as clear as the night they were uttered. "Don't blame Briggs, Dip. It wasn't his fault. Some jerk crossed the road right in front of him. He yelled to me to look out. It wasn't his fault." Then Wilf had fainted dead-away and was unconscious for most of two days. Wilf, he also remembered, had come out of high school and went right into the army, Korea on the horizon like a dirty word and some of his pals over there mixing with the Chinese.

The night in front of the church, just before Wilf left for the army, came back to Dip. "It's better me than some of them, Dip." He motioned to some of their pals down the street waiting for the dance to get over and the girls to come out. They were making crazy noises, making gestures at the sky, then in sudden embarrassment cooling abruptly as though people were looking at them. "I'm more ready than they are." The stance was not bluster; it was concrete.

And Wilf was right. All of 20 at the time, Wilf came home with a Bronze Star and a Purple Heart with a cluster pinned on his chest. Never once had Dip ever heard Wilf Gamin talk about his service in the army, about Korea, about firefights, about the Chinese. And it was at that exact instant that Dip Connors realized full well that everything the man knew was most likely entered into his journals. Dip was willing to bet the whole Korean scene was included in the journals, every battle or engagement no matter the size, every comrade at his side, every remnant scar; it would have been the way the man did it. Rather than breathing it, boasting of it, he had applied it with ink.

And if there was anything out of the past concerning Shanklin Garuf, Dip was willing to bet it was there, part of history, entered by hand, in Wilf Gamin's journals, in one or more of the known 62 journals the man had created.

Dip asked Wilf to step aside, into a corner of the yacht club. "I need some talk with you, Wilf. It's damned important to me and to Cap, but I need you agreeing up front with it. Maybe I'm coming at you odd or you might think out of reason, perhaps an invasion of privacy, but I'd like to take a peek at your journals. I want to know if there are any leads there I can follow up. Any wild ass connections you've forgotten that might give me a clue, maybe something trivial to you but a sparkler in my eyes." The first sense of imploration came from his puckered lips. "God, man, I have to start someplace. I'm getting nowhere as it is." He looked back over his shoulder at the gang of them, like a cluster of warm pleasant ashes from an old fire. "No need to share what I know with anybody. Strictly twixt you and me." Dip's hand fell on Wilf Gamin's shoulder as strong and as sure as a handclasp might have been between the pair.

Wilf nodded. "You're the boss, Dip. I don't play games with that stuff. Don't share it because it's mine, even though all of them are in it." He nodded his head back over his shoulder to the boatyard gang. "That's most of my life right there, Dip. Just about most of it. That takes some kind of appreciation. If you think going through my stuff can help, be my guest, but it's all between you and me. There are a few observations I'd rather not share, if you know what I mean." He nodded over his shoulder again. Dip could feel the robust squeeze of promise, demanding promise, in Wilf Gamin's words. "And then again, there are things in there I can hardly remember writing, never mind the thing happening itself. It's weird but it's like I've been a stranger my whole life."

Wilf turned his face fully to Dip. Deepness came with his voice and that sudden depth filled with both reach and annunciation. "You ever feel you're not quite what you think you are, Dip? Ever get that feeling down in your boots that somebody else is wearing them? I mean, honest to God, do you?"

The most honest facial expression Detective Dip Connors ever saw came to him from the quiet man standing beside him, looking back at a group of fast friends, looking back at his whole life. At once, from some distant point within or without, he was not sure of the point of origin, the small town detective had a sense of unknown proportions smashing through him. And he knew a sudden clarity; that a true observation had come from the mouth of a quiet man he never would figure for such a conviction. Here was an Adam and Eve man, a representative man, the core of his pals locked into his own being; he was one and all. The thought staggered the veteran detective yet he could feel a resolve as hard as a rock.

Three days later, cored to the task, oblivious to all else around him, Dip was digging. *His handwriting is so difficult, probably thinks it's coded he does, or wants any reader to think so, but I have fathomed it.* Dip Connors muttering under bright light working hard, three days at it beginning to take its toll, being assessed.

He read. He screwed his eyes down to the vast pages. *Damn,* he muttered, *I thought I knew everything.* The lights lit up the back of his head, the icons of men at the world, of it. *I thought I knew this band of brothers, this cement between men. I thought I knew! Oh my God, I thought I knew!*

He was whirling through all their lives, privy to pains and glories, and he knew it, as if he were in on a birth. *Fragments of other lives whirling through my mind. The serials of them, the scraps of bark. Elements. Pure and simple, the elements!* He paused. *There they are,* he muttered again, *caught forever in the rhythm of the river, subject to the tide, the coming and the going, and I am now part of that rhythm, Wilf and me.*

Salvi's mother, in the dead of night, the Calabrese dictate hard on her soul, swinging the razor on her husband's ear. "Sumnabitch, sumnabitch! No more you play the waitress. No more you bring her smell inna my kitchen. Bastid! Now you hear me ever and ever!"

Before him, stripped bare, was Brittan losing a son and his wife in the one accident. The drunk oblivious until early morning in jail of what he had done. Wilf had plied it with his own pain, the words about Brittan, the love the man knew and espoused. They came across the pages to Dip, seven pages damp as dew. He felt the caricature of the drunk, heard the sound of metals impacting souls, and knew at last the lingering pain on Brittan's face, where a pair of lips held forever an unannounced curse. Dip knew Brittan as he had never known him. And so, he knew Wilf.

Then Bent Crilson leaped his humanity into his eyes; limping through the Death March at Bataan, throwing his life aside with a dash into the jungle, finding escape. *It must have been a secret night between the two of them,* Dip thought, *for I've never heard word one from Bent about his time in the Philippines.* Dip could picture the two of them, Bent and Wilf, late, at the back end of the bar, letting out a lifetime of secrets without an audience in attendance, *Taps* coming out of a Luzon jungle as faint as silent airs. Dip thought he saw a Philippine moon, low, against a tattered cloud, hanging its paleness over them.

It is all staggering, this core of revelation, this endless exposure, and it finds revulsion in the measures of my soul, this personal affront, this breach of sibling parapets. How could Wilf stand to make such a record? How could he bear so much pain and so much glory? What manner of man could contain all this knowledge and never, never once, spill his guts, air out the whole world of being? Oh, what courage, he thinks. *What resistance. What boon companionship. What dread.*

He is crowded by this knowledge; his breast beats.

"She was pregnant," Muckles said, "and tried to rid herself of it. God, man, I killed her. It was all my fault." A hundred years of memory, it seems, collapsed down on Dip as he read. Sweet but revolutionary Carrie Thurbitt at the turn of the river, her dress snagged on the bank by an old car bumper, a classmate in her last turn at water. Out of the dim past he remembered the ceremony, knew the exact temperature of the chill wind at Riverside Cemetery coming through the trees and up the narrow avenues as Carrie was put down to rest, her aborted child someplace in the other world. Muckles to this day toting that barge-like weight across his back almost fifty years worth.

Dip Connors at a library of lives.

There were reams of revelations; some made him bow his head, some creased him with a smile, and then, on his third late night, deep in the journal begun in January of 1996 he sat straight up in his chair. A small remark, an aside of sorts, that painted the scene of animosity, of threat, around Shanklin Garuth. Dip shuddered to think it might have been said by one of the boatyard gang, and when he turned the page the culprit was named, a Townie but not one of *them*. A known bad-ass guy that had given Dip fits a number of times. But not one of *them*! Not one of *them*!

It was, he knew, a place to start.

All it took, after reading the journals of a quiet man, was for Detective Dip Connors, Saugus stalwart, to start his walk down the front walkway of the troublesome Townie, who broke and ran at the sight of the bulldog detective descending on him.

And Wilf Gamin, ever quiet, never said anything about what he couldn't remember writing, not wanting anybody to know that he had already forgotten some names. *That* was terror enough.

Man with Inner Movies

Long-time widower Jake Adamo, cop for thirty-seven years, Little League coach for more than thirty of those years, mere months from an early retirement, his last ten years as a detective, believing his body had finally let him down, screwed his mind down to the smallest detail of what appeared to be his final case on the job. This was one of his kids now in trouble, one of the elite kids when they had made a run at a national championship back in the good old days, his second baseman Bobby "Bobo" Carnes. Bobo was a tough kid who'd stop a grounder with his mouth if he had to, a brilliant student, a smart business man now while still so young. And in the far reach of town, a man, a near recluse, dead, garroted with a strange weapon, one Jake had never seen before. And Bobo in the mix.

Jake, it was well known in local police circles, could go over his cases the way he replayed the old games, a whole game at a time, each pitch, each hit or play by one of his fielders standout or routine, or an enemy strikeout, the ball coming back to the pitcher, the new look at the new parameters. Once in a while he could hear the bell that Bobo's mother rang at every game, like a charm at work, out of the mysterious Southwest. He had brought that capacity of memory and imagination fully functional into police work. "They are," he once told a friend, "my inner movies." With astounding clarity he could run movies of cases nine or ten years in the past. He was a cop's museum.

He reran the Bobo film time and again long into the night as he sat on his porch on the side of a hill, sights and sounds coming to him as if by magic from a few words of the principals, sometimes fewer words than he wanted. Bobo was still brown-eyed but bright, with an outlandishly handsome smile, complexion out of the southwest for sure, tanned, darker than friends and teammates, somewhat contagious in his outlook. Like the flow of a game should have been or could have been, Jake was able to fill in holes the way they ought to be from those few words. He could measure against perfection, a thesis on life, a thesis on people.

We were at the Topsfield Fair, Jake, Bobo had said. *It was a harmless night out, the fairgrounds loaded with color and noise:*

Young engineer and nouveau designer Roberto "Bobo" Carnes lost his wallet traipsing through the Topsfield Fairgrounds on an October evening, air bright and unrelenting with an edge of ax in it en route from the north country, smells rich and pungent throughout the tents and barns and outbuildings of the fair as if ripeness was a sense of measure and success. Steaming vendor wagons seemed heaped upon one another in the business fray, casting themselves through the crowded ways.

I had it and then I didn't have it:

Bobo, taking all in through valid senses, thought his loss just a plain hundred-dollar loss, for that's all that he had tucked away in the wallet folds, plus a few loose dollars. Never spent much, never carried much. Lavish restaurants, sporty cars, spectacular women had no serious play for him. "Been there, done that," he'd say to himself halfheartedly, as if a casual truth had been spoken. Yet for such a small exchange of wallet contents, he had no idea what was coming at him. Full bore.

Things have been going good for me, Jake:

New patents of his were sound and firmly planted and business going better than anticipated. One proposed design and patent in the back of his mind, a veritable leech sucking into his brain, was *a now and forever gadget.* Simple it was, like a paper clip or clothespin, or the clichéd mousetrap, and with it once perfected, said from the outset, he'd be set for life. The small mechanical spread was never far from his center of thought. From his genius Mexican mother, caught up in the rigors and throes of manual labor all the damn dusty and dry way from her sixth year on this harsh Earth, he'd received a gift of acute object adaptation; for a single object he could find many uses, spread its intent, apply it elsewhere, those novel uses bursting in him to be free. A genius at it he was, possibilities continually erupting at the back of his head like fireworks, strange gadgets and odd contraptions clutching, grasping, getting footholds in his brain matter. His head was a lab, a tool room, a closet, a fix-it shop, a stocked garage, an overflowing bench at the foot of the cellar stairs waiting for the overhead light to go on, hands to touch things.

What the hell is a hundred bucks:

The lost wallet, for that matter, had no serious grasp on his mind, inert it was, no moving and tactile parts, no intricacies or puzzlement, no concept at challenge, mere representative of other conditions, passive at the most. Initially, at discovery of the lost wallet, he shrugged his shoulders. "Had it, lost it," he muttered, a wave off.

Only a few pictures of Hannah, Jake:

At the fairgrounds, a mix of October color was resident in the trees along the Ipswich River and in one sentinel red maple in particular, a sweet breath in the air and a sense of exultant fall coming with it. Late afternoon sun had dropped its incendiaries into trees along the river and splendor danced its ignition as far as the eye could see. Bobo, for a good hour caught between the tree blaze and the fair's smells, had carried a light jacket before donning it. That's when the wallet was first missed, no longer zipped into a jacket pocket. A couple of credit cards he could recount, along with his driver's license, a folded hundred dollar bill tucked under a leather separator, a few pictures of his sister Hannah, and little else. He could picture her, Hard Hannah! "Hannah was to be borne, to say the least," he admitted on a regular basis. "Life," he remembered his mother used to say, "is a road with many obstacles." Perhaps his tall sister Hannah was one of those bumps on the main highway. Attitude, in varied instances, had to be a bump.

You remember Hannah, Jake:

As he did quite often, Bobo thought of Hannah when the loss was discovered, the way she could unnerve him, test his Mexican calmness. To be borne, he thought. He'd bear her again. It was his way. He'd bug her for more pictures, it was his due and calling, and it would be a task, the way she held back small favors, putting up that wall he sometimes believed was resignation, then at times nothing more than sass or impudence. He worked at making blood thicker than water. It was not an easy task. Even at the odd roots, she was family. When he'd asked her a year earlier to go on a trip with him, a week free on the West Coast, she had said, "I'm not sharing in your spoils, Bobo. I told you that before! Get off the case!" Even before that he'd noticed a distinct drifting, what he assumed was a pittance of jealousy. There was a status less talked about would be better.

Hannah, to most eyes he agreed, was somewhat plain, but she, like some of the women that Bobo had known or come in contact with, maintained a spectacular body hidden to most of those eyes. Often he wondered how many women were like that, like Hard Hannah, somehow lost to the casual eye, daily buried in their selection of clothes, making the wrong turn in life, turning a different page, at odds with notice, with attraction. Perhaps it was disdain or the way Hannah dressed: woolly, somber, somewhat down east in tone, as if ready for the weather or what might come of it in the next damn breath. Despite what he hoped for in her outlook, she did dress to match her personality. It was the obverse of his mother's Southwestern dress, though that too was ready for the weather, the desert, the sudden and harsh calls of the land. It was the way he also knew his long-departed mother to be, careful and cautious, ready for anything, taking life head on yet predictable in her steady assurances. Nudity was for god or husband, she believed, and those two at times interchangeable.

One time we figured out you had been listening to us all the time, Jake, every damn word we ever said, and you sat at one end of the bench or the back of the bus and read lips! We had no secrets from you:

Reflection grabbed hold of Bobo, coming down long pastures of memories, green and unfenced and running to an old horizon. As young teenagers he and a few pals had often rated women, especially older women by at least a few years, on the merits of their bodies under the clutch of clothes. They played guessing games at breast and cup sizes, hip spreads, crotch colors and conditions, buttock spans, how thighs so elongated could be so elegant and so attractive against the span of a simple dark material of dress or skirt. The press of it! The shape behind it! Oh, all the world and glory and amen! Amazement and revelation, in turn, came upon them along with feelings that flooded their veins, promised happenings sooner than later, great hopeful breakouts in the offing, small realizations. The eternal wait, though, was delicious. "Where there's smoke, there's friggin' fire, friggin' fire!" his pal Paints Brown would say. They stared. They ogled. They snickered. And they delighted again and again in those small revelations they gave to one another.

Nicky Redding came back to him in a flash, as if he had never gone down to the sea in that stupid ship, crying into the back of his hand, his dark eyes of ever-lasting Mediterranean pain shut for the moment, "Oh, the bush, guys! The bush!" and he'd lick the back of his hand like a vanilla cone had melted all over it and they'd be in hysterics. And Nicky wasn't the clown of the group, he was the reader. He had come to them time and again talking about the Mound of Venus and the Seven Cities of Cibola, the moving support, the bastion of all mankind, "where the rich get richer and the poor make up for all the difference." He could qualify anything: "The bush grows on a hill, guys, the top of the friggin' world. Like Rome was on a hill." They laughed and they waited and made pictures in their minds, sitting on cement with their backs against the field house brick wall and out in front of them the endless parade of girls passing from game to game, tush and bush afield.

You knew we had crushes on a few teachers, the young ones, and you knew why:

Teachers though were their favorites, snatched up in the gathering of attention, caught in well-lighted doorways, against a May or June window silhouetted by a superior sunlight, retrieving something from a bottom desk draw or reaching across a desktop. Naked, he and his buddies constantly thought, was best, was illustrious, was the end-all. For their efforts they had perfected a pretty good eye for hidden women. Hannah fit that eye to a T. Hidden Hannah, oh, Hard Hannah. Now a new friend to Bobo and her, Jack Kilrain, had taken her on a couple of dates. Bobo had been hopeful for Hannah and the timing seemed good. Perhaps he'd get her to smile more often, as if she'd ever smile when her brother was about. He had borne her best he could, and mouthed that acceptance under his breath too often.

I met this guy fishing, on the Ipswich, Jake, near Bradley Palmer State Park, and he knew some hidden spots, and shared them easily and he ends up dating Hannah:

Fair noises loomed all around, and the chatter and the impersonal interplay of strangers. Sausage and pepper and onion smells crowded the air, as well as donut and cider aromas. With the tasty smells came the sense of newly strewn hay, fresh manure droppings, a full mix of animal and vegetable airs from the barns and showrooms. He and his new pal and Hannah's recent date, Jack Kilrain, went back over known ground looking for the wallet or a finder's commotion, without any luck.

A few months earlier he had met Jack on the Ipswich River as their canoes passed each and they shared insider information on a few good fishing spots. Jack had volunteered first, his bright face all smiles, his eyes full of river light, one of those Pepsodent faces out of a magazine ad. "Go back upstream from the bridge at Bradley Palmer State Park, a few hundred yards or so," said with a shoulder shrug and a full smile, "around one main turn and one old blow-down that's bleached near white and been there for years, and you'll find where Pye Brook empties into the Ipswich, coming down through a sea of grass. Get your canoe up in there, up in the high grass and reeds you can't see over, though there's not much turn-around room. You might shake a hundred birds loose of their nests. I hit a good half dozen healthy brookies there last week, a couple of rainbows, and left some for the next trip. Maybe next weekend. Haven't seen anybody up in there for years." His own age, likable, a fisherman alone in a canoe, Bobo immediately thought him pleasant and warm, always having room for new friends.

You know how fishermen are:

Bobo in turn leaked information on a few spots of his own, especially the one just below the fairgrounds they were now on, the first turn above the old Iron Bridge. Hell, he had kept his word to an older friend for close to ten years. Time was ripe for new hands, new conquests. The water lapping against the side of his canoe, a stillness settling down on the end of day, he wondered if he had seen Jack before, in surroundings just as pleasant, there being something familiar and warm about him.

At the barn where the horse-pulling contests were about to start, Jack said, "Why don't you call the cops or fair officials. Perhaps someone will turn it in." His hand was on Bobo's shoulder, sort of urging him.

"I don't think there's much chance of that," Bobo countered. "Not with a single hundred folded away. I'll cancel my credit cards. There's just two of them from what I remember. No problem. Might be a Lost and Found around here, though, and we'll let them know."

The night of extreme odors and sights pressed on and the two forgot the wallet and had a go at the rich spill of sausages and cider and later a heavy share of chicken chop suey in a roll. Jack Kilrain paid with ease and laughter. Already he had taken Hannah out on a couple of expensive dates and there was promise of more. An affinity was warming strongly between the two men, Bobo thinking Jack was exactly what Hannah needed in this life, always smiling, light on his face, a dimple on his chin, teeth so perfect they could have been made. During the evening he admitted he had some kind of feelings for Hannah, so far unexplainable. Would he be just what the doctor ordered for Hannah? The next morning Bobo canceled all his credit cards.

Then I looked up the street as I'm going off to work and the cops are there:

Three mornings later, as he was about to drive to his office and shop in Danvers, a police car pulled in behind him and two policemen stepped out. Immediately Bobo recognized Jake Adamo, now in plainclothes after a burden of years on the street. Jake had aged, was heavier, looked slower but wiser.

"Hi, Jake," Bobo yelled. "You guys on business or social?" The look on Jake's face he read almost too quickly. "What's the matter, Jake? You have that old 3-and-2-bases-loaded look." At the back of his neck an odd sensation, almost electrical, told Bobo that nothing was going to be funny.

With a quick frown, Jake's face agreed, eyes clouded, large teeth biting into the cigar, one hand waving hapless. "I have a problem, Bobo," he said, neither apologetic nor condescending, dark eyes fuller now of shadow and honest concern. "There's been a crime committed, pretty serious. One of your credit cards found at the scene. You got any explanations that might fit that?"

Jake's voice was hard and gruff, an all-work voice with years of cigars riding in it, and thousands of night hours of patrol. *Who, where, what* was not offered up. An unlit cigar hung like a comma from his mouth. His hair was thin, his neck heavy in a button-down collar, the paunch more rotund than ever. Jake had been a hard-line coach, no bullshit about him when it came to parents, going straight at them right to the core of a problem. Bobo suddenly remembered Billy Cantella's mother coming to the bench in a game years earlier, embarrassing the hell out of Billy after inept Billy had not started in right field for six straight games. Jake had spoken loud and clear, "Lady, you stay away from my goddamn bench and I'll guarantee you I'll stay out of your goddamn kitchen!"

Bobo wanted to laugh his answer to Jake's question but didn't, the odd sensation, still electric, still on him. "I lost my wallet at the fairgrounds the other night. Had a couple of my credit cards in it. Some old pictures of Hannah (almost sounding apologetic, he thought), a hundred bucks. Did it show up someplace?" Then, accepting the odd feeling telling him something else, he said, "What happened with this crime? Someone hurt?" The electricity was like a special circuit had been rigged just for him.

Jake ignored part of Bobo's reply. "What kind of credit cards, Bobo? You remember?" As if that was important, and Bobo thinking Jake was just being "official." Jake put the old unlit cigar in his mouth. "Know what brand they were?" Bobo thought for sure the bases were loaded and Jake had no idea of who to use as a pinch hitter. That look of Jake's would never change. He could call it perplexity, but wasn't sure it would fit.

"I don't know. I figure I had two of them in my wallet, but canceled four cards, just to be sure." Bobo knew it didn't sound too good. "I don't remember which two were there. I'm not sure of the issue or the cut-off dates. I have thrown new ones away by mistake. I don't use them very much. Only on trips. I really don't know what they were. You know me, Jake, Frugal Freddie. Always been that way. I'm not much for the hot stuff." Somehow his voice sounded empty, unsure of its own source, hollow all the way from where it came.

Jake's answer was quick and out of character. "This is hot stuff, Bobo. Extremely hot stuff." Bobo thought Jake looked as if one of his kids had been thrown out at the plate, when he said, "I'm afraid you'll have to come down to the station. There are some questions." All the old days had diminished in value, the game winning double in the last of the seventh off there in Connecticut in a championship game long gone down the tube, times had changed.

Bobo heard the details: A man in the next town had been strangled with a twist of wire tied to a strange spring arrangement. Death was immediate. Most immediate! The coroner said he had never seen such a contraption. "Dropped over his head, probably when he got out of his car in the garage. Bango! Snapped into his neck like a shot. Didn't even need to be held. No marks on his body, not grabbed by the arms. This man was not subdued and then strangled. He was killed quicker than you can imagine." Then the coroner shook his head. "Never seen the likes of it. It's new-fangled. It's impressive." The victim was not rich, not well known, was in fact somewhat reclusive. Few people, it was assessed, would miss him. But he was dead!

Death was fixed at just after midnight. Bobo said he was in his small shop, alone. It was where he probably spent five nights a week, working on his new pieces; a new design for a wheelbarrow, a new toaster with a vastly different set-up, a carburetor he believed would start a revolution. Nobody could vouch he was there on the night of the murder. Later, when police searched his shop one of the things they took away with them was a spring. It proved to be the same type as employed in the murder weapon.

Jake, visibly uncomfortable, later sat with Bobo at the station. "No ideas, Bobo? Not a one?"

"Jeez, Jake, how could I have any ideas? I didn't even know the guy. Don't think I ever saw him."

"Well, it's small comfort for you, I guess, Bobo, but I don't think you did it. You got too much on your platter. You've always had that. The mystery is I think someone's trying to set you up, if you ask me. But we have to cover all this ground. Like the spring we found in your shop. Has to be explained. Somebody knows something about you, that's plain to see."

"Jake," Bobo said, "I bought two dozen of those springs at that shop in Salem, the one burned down last year. Where the two firemen got hurt. I can account for all but one. I don't know what happened to it, but I sure as hell didn't use it to kill somebody."

"Anybody strange been in your shop?" The cigar at Jake's lips hung limp as a flower in October's mouth, and his eyes filled with distance.

Perhaps, Bobo thought, *he's really tired of the job, looking closer at retirement, might be Naples, Florida I see in there or Marco Island.* "Only a couple of vendor reps a few weeks ago," he offered, "from out of state. Nobody else. Not a soul." He shook his head. "I don't want anybody in there when I'm not there. It's always been that way. My sister doesn't even get in there if I'm not around."

Jake filed that qualification, and then said, "How's it going?"

"I'm sitting on a keg of dynamite, Jake. One of my rigs is going to take off like a rocket. I've got some solid queries on it."

"Who benefits besides you, Bobo?"

"My sister Hannah gets everything if anything happens to me, if that's what you mean. Like if I die or get incarcerated for a long spell. You getting into that drift?"

You know what Hannah's like, Jake:

Jake had a way of turning things aside, relegating them to unimportant status. "What kind of relationship is she in?"

"She's dated a few guys, but not many. Doesn't like to mix too much. Been out with a pal of mine a couple of times. Jack Kilrain. He was with me the night I lost my wallet."

Jake didn't turn this one aside. "He ever been in your shop?" Jake had a way of trying to be bland and unexcited, but the manipulation of the cigar gave him away; it bobbed like a nerve ending.

"Nope, not once. Casual doesn't get anybody in there, Jake. It's the way I play it."

Jake looked off to a corner of the room. "All we have, Bobo, is your sister and your new buddy. So far as we know there's nobody else in the mix. Can't think of anybody who doesn't like your ass for some godforsaken reason?"

Bobo thought Jake could get *unbland* too, in a hurry. "Not a one, Jake."

"I've learned a lot on this job, Bobo. One of the things I've learned is that someplace, somewhere, for whatever reason, there's someone who doesn't like your ass. It can be old as the hills, the reason for such hatred. You never know where it's coming from. But it's there like the handle on a piss pot."

"You mean someone, for years, could have been waiting to set me up, to settle an old score? Simple as that?"

"Or waiting for you to get prime." Jake looked off into the corner again, the shadow in his eyes yet, the cigar clinched in his lips but almost moving like a heart's wave chart.

Been out with a pal of mine a couple of times. Jack Kilrain. He was with me the night I lost my wallet:

Jake, shortly thereafter and unknown to Bobo, bird-dogged Jack Kilrain on a few odd occasions. On one such trip Jake came across a steely-eyed acquaintance of Kilrain's that spooked him. The pair didn't match up in any manner, not in age or clothes or manners.

A profile artist, he knew, would never put the two together in a hundred years, yet here they were, swinging their feet over the sea wall at Kings Beach down in Lynn as if they were long lost pals, sharing a bag of French fries, an October breeze, a hunk of sunshine. Jake took his jacket and tie off, dropped them onto the front seat of his car, put on an old sweater found in the trunk and rolled up the sleeves. Sauntering by the pair as if on his own stroll for salt air, his ears were cocked wide, the tide music humming in his ears, the spill of waves, the monotone of traffic.

"So your buddy's going to be a millionaire, huh? Looks kind of dark as far as I can see, one of them Wetbacks I'll bet, come up here to rape the land. Now don't go getting pissed off at me, but I saw you guys at the fair. I was tossing hay for a few drinks and a place for my head for the night. Got a few drinks and a meal out of it. They don't give a sucker a break even in those places claim they're getting back to the land. More crap for fodder, if you ask me."

"I get the idea you've been watching closer than I thought. That's way out of line. You tell anybody about him? Somebody got on his case."

Jake had gotten that much! He wanted to slow down dramatically, but feared doing so. Bobo was a good kid. Always had been. Some of his teammates and other kids he had coached had turned out real shitty, but he had stopped worrying about that a long time ago. If he stopped to retie his shoelaces, play a hesitating game, it would be a giveaway. He kept walking, reached the end of the sea wall and sat down. All the way out to the dim gray horizon he looked, watching a tanker or some large ship almost disappear over that demarcation. The double Bobo had hit in one championship game had almost given them the title. All these years later he could still feel the thrill at the back of his head. Sometimes it made him breathe heavy; it was as close as he'd ever come, him and his endless dreams about the World Series. When he turned to look back at the two men, he saw Kilrain place an envelope on the rim of the sea wall, spin around on his butt and walk off down the wide sea walk. In a red Corvette, practically noiseless for being so red, he spun away from the beach.

Jake watched Jack Kilrain's seedy looking companion open the envelope and count a goodly sum of money. Jake could feel all the options being narrowed. He was suddenly sure that the connecting link would be Bobo's sister Hannah. This nondescript acceptor of funds was tied to Bobo's sister and her share of any forthcoming will, and any forthcoming incarceration of her brother. So that meant her new boyfriend, and Bobo's new pal, Jack Kilrain. Jake wondered how many ways he could put the screws to a devious plan. The options, he believed, were limitless.

Jake began a tail on Kilrain's seedy pal. Later in the day, after noting little, finding nothing, he put Ashton Croft on the tail. Ashton was good, cool, inventive.

Later in the night, Ashton called Jake. "I got this jamoke inside Bobo's shop. Walks up to the door, takes out a key, opens the door and walks in. You'd think he owned the place. Shall I grab him when he comes out or keep the tail going?"

"Hell, we can't get him for breaking and entering. He had a damn key, but we can get him for unlawful entry I'd guess. He doesn't have permission to be in there. Keep on the track. See what he does, where he goes, what he carries off with him. If he brings something to Kilrain, we want to know how and what it is, how it's going to be used in an another crime. If that's his purpose for this entry. He's apparently the guy who took the spring out of there, the one did the other guy in."

You know what Hannah's like, Jake:

Then Jake had one of those surprise decisions that had been ground into his life since the very first baseball game he had ever managed; whatever came and went in this it had to go through or by or around Hannah. Paying her a call would be a choice option. And not letting Bobo know what he was up to was just as good. She answered his knock.

"This is a real surprise, Jake. Don't think I've talked to you in twenty years or so, though I've seen you plying your trade, read about you every so often. Is this about the mess around Bobo? Something is real shitty there." Her face was bland, mushroomy, eyes holding back light. He bet she could be a real bitch. So damn different from Bobo.

Jake suddenly remembered how plain Hannah had been in those early years. And she was still carrying that same look on her face, like oatmeal a day old. Yet something about the way her housecoat rode on her more than ample hips threw that line of thought out the window in a hurry. Her breasts, easy to see, had prospered greatly, were willing antagonists in the clutch of white flannel. She was, he thought, probably an animal in the sack, but you'd have to bag her to get her there.

"Murder's never easy, Hannah. This one's as messy as it can get, being Bobo's one of my old team. He's quite something, that brother of yours. No way he did what happened. Bobo's clean as a whistle, as they say." He watched for any reaction. The reaction was his; Jeezus, he thought, her jugs are almost out and she doesn't give a shit, is unconscious about it, or she's using them. No two ways about is, she's an animal in bed but still a bitch. The last conclusion let him get past her.

"I heard the weapon was a piece from his shop," she said. "Is that true or is it being made up? How can that really be connected to Bobo?" No lines moved on her face, no expression rode with her words.

Her legs were so long he bet she could do the high hurdles for the track team. He could almost see where they ended up. "There's some speculation that it was taken out of his place to put Bobo on the spot." He might as well get right to it. Her hands were in the pockets of the housecoat and she might have been ready to stretch, so visible was she, a cat stretching, a thing of the jungle. The eyes looking at him were coming out of a long darkness, another night. Jake swore there was an odor of sex in the air, biting, near saline.

"That doesn't sound too pleasant. Are you implying something

that's not been said yet? You saying something about me, Jake?"
The D cups were loose, the legs longer than he thought, her eyes
suddenly full of that old mystery that had long passed him by. The
thought came to him that she was plying for a trade-off, making a
move.

*I met this guy fishing, on the Ipswich, and he knew some hidden
spots, and shared them easily and he ends up dating Hannah:*

"Tell me about your new friend Jack Kilrain and his pal I see with
him down the beach on a couple of occasions. You know the
other guy, kinda seedy looking, maybe looking for a place to sleep
tonight, might be begging for his next meal. Know him?" He was
thinking that there was more to Bobo than he thought, that he
sure must have had a lot of patience to put up with such a sister. If
Bobo could have killed anybody it probably would be this sister
of his.

   "How would I know him, Jake? I've only known Jack for a
short time. Is there a connection here? You saying something I'm
just guessing at?"

   "Look, Hannah," he said, "as far as I'm concerned, the only
connections we have are you and your new friend, Jack Kilrain.
Nothing else's in the mix, not yet. How did you meet him? He
ever been here?"

You know what Hannah's like, Jake:

"I don't get too many guys looking my way, Jake. Out there I
know I'm different than in here. I can relax here, be myself. Out
there I can't. You must know people like that." Her honesty struck
him and her hands came out of her pockets, the housecoat was
drawn close, Jake thinking all offers were now off the table. "I'm
out shopping one day, half a dozen stores and half a dozen times
this good looking guy is around. Not messing around, but there.
Most times not looking at me, his back to me in a few places, but

present in a positive sense, if you know what I mean. Sometimes it gets kind of electric, touching you in different places, being real. It got to me, it got to me real good, so I keep looking for him, extending my shopping, feeling a little heat in my pants, to be honest with you. It'd been a while for me; we all have inordinate hungers at times, but real. Suddenly we're bumping into each other and he's looking in my eyes and looking me over and we're talking and warm feelings in the air and we're having a coffee and this guy is burning a hole right through me. I hadn't felt like that in a long while, Jake, and he says to me out of the blue, 'Hannah, you like oral sex?' Just like that, straight out, no bullshitting around, and his eyes are wide and his smile is so fucking beautiful and I'm so far past hungry for it he must have read my soul. Before you know it we had a few drinks and then we're in his car in the parking garage, off in a corner, one of those sun shades over the windshield and we're swapping favors in the back seat, just like we were kids again."

One time we figured out you had been listening to us all the time, Jake, every damn word we ever said, and you sat at one end of the bench or the back of the bus and read lips! We had no secrets from you:

Now plain Hannah, oatmeal-face Hannah, was a live wire right in the room. Jake agreed it was raw sex he smelled when he first walked in. This girl was a hidden woman. He remembered Bobo and the other kids talking about it years ago. He'd always known there were such types and never met one, not like this. The curve of her neck showed elegance he had missed. He wondered how much else he had missed. Not the breasts or the hips or the legs. There was always the promise of so much more. "He ever been here, Hannah?"

"Oh, sure," she smiled. "Even that first day. I'd dropped my pocketbook in the car, spilled some stuff, he picks it up and drives me home and drops me in front. I get to my door and I have no keys. The Super let me in. An hour later Jack's knocking at my door. He's got my keys, waving them in his hand. Jeezus, but he looks good and we go right back at it. Spent the day catching up on lost times I did. It was marvelous. He mentioned marriage but in a passing way, but like openers, like future. I don't get many chances like that, Jake. Said he found the keys in the car when he got to his place, lives in Belmont, came right back with them."

"You have a key to Bobo's shop on your keychain?" Jake had stopped looking for surprises, his mind seeing this creature in the back seat of a car, swapping favors. Her face had lost some of that oatmeal quality, her eyes were dark and full of hope, a whole sea of hope that must have had endless tides, her lips promising to part, to be moist, and her complete life suddenly exposed to him.

"Yes, I do."

One full scenario of crime, not only how it was done and but why it was done, all the parts of the script, came to Jake Adamo as Hannah started to unfold, first with slight trembling and hand-shaking, then a spill of tears falling across her cheeks. He wanted to reach out for her, even as he heard himself telling Bobo there was a reason behind everything that had gone on, from his meeting Jack on the river, their instant friendship, the move on Hannah, the keys Jack had probably made copies of in a hurry, the future.

Her eyes, wet as they were, were wider than before, suddenly much wider. "You saying he used me, Jake? The loving we did was just to get at Bobo? It wasn't quick and real like he said?" The tall, usually passive woman, the bland creature he had known since she was a kid, almost collapsed in his arms.

You know what Hannah's like, Jake: Oh, god, yes!

He held her, felt her against him all down his body, knew the hidden woman she was, knew now that it was too late for him, the kind of creature he had always known could have existed for him. In that frozen second, her breasts heavy on him, the animal length of her exacted measurements from him, unexpected measurements, and then a valid core of memory. Bobo's bases-clearing double way down in Connecticut came back to him; how he cornered so lightly and effortlessly at first base on the inside of the bag taking that quick turn to a double, the slide into second and his triumphant leap, the high throw in from the cut-off man, the bright sunshine on Bobo's face as he triggered a finger at the bench, the sound of the rally cries in his ears. It was all there for the playing, playing out just as quick as this murder on hand, just as clear, just like a bell was ringing behind him, somewhere in the stands.

Home from the Dead

E arl Chatsby, six years after he ceased being a father for real, felt an odd distinction coming into his place of being. The newspaper for the moment loomed an idle bundle in his lap, the way it stayed weighty and rolled and unread. Walls of the kitchen widened, and the room took in more air. He could feel the huge gulp of it. The coffee pot was perking loudly its 6 a.m. sound and the faucet drip, fixed three nights earlier at Melba's insistence, had hastened again its freedom, the discord highly audible. Atop the oil cloth over the kitchen table the mid-May sun continued dropping its slanting hellos, allowing them to spread the room into further colors. Yet to this day he cannot agree to what happened first, the front porch shadow at the window coming vaguely visible in a corner of his eye, a familiar shadow, or the slight give-away trod heard from the porch floor, that too familiar, the board loose it seemed forever and abraded by Melba's occasional demands to fix it.

Change, evermore to be remembered, was at hand.

In one desperate moment, before trying to make up his mind between the selection of the shadow or the footstep as being the initial impact, Earl Chatsby ran his engine of recall. Morning crowded him into the past with a push so harsh and thorough his head spun atop his shoulders. The fleetness of crowded memory was punishing. He saw that other sun, the high sky with endless blue, that other day itself crowded with so many small glimpses of personal data that he shuddered. In a pale reflection there was Paul Moffie, peering out his front room window across the street; Paul had leaped back so many times after his death with a constant apology that he had neglected to say goodbye to Purly. It had happened hundreds of times, that ghostly re-appearance becoming Paul's legacy.

Purly's steps that last morning had a pause to them, an intricate measurement, as he came down from his bedroom, the sound coming off as a slowed-down metronome full of careful cadence. Earl had measured that tread too, that slow tread, knowing the hesitation in it, the built-in delay in getting on in the world as though it was all visible to his son, seeing what was out there in front of him. That other day was also a May day, and still holding its breath, a treasure to be kept and hidden and only used when absolutely needed for the spirit. Earl once tried to categorize that treasure and only found plausible options, forced memory or forceful memory, and then he tossed them each aside.

Earl looked up and saw his son's uniform pressed so clearly and squarely that Melba must have outdone herself. The corporal stripes appeared as sharp as razor blades on the sleeves of his army shirt, what he called his suntans or summer issue. The pants, bloused into his boots, seemed sheet metal stiff as he stepped away from the stairs, stiff enough to break apart.

"Looks like Mum honed you up on a razor strop, Purly. Them pants appear like she had them corrugated." Pride rode a small flush in Earl Chatsby's face as he looked upon his son so near to departure. That he was going off to the war was a hidden fact for the merest second, and then it slammed home, overtaking and overpowering the pride he had felt flushing him so deeply inside it must have shown outside. The felt redness was proof. A knock began in his chest, a dreadful music marking him, sighing, not singing, as mean as a flag waving in front of his eyes. It was almost wanton from then on, that feeling. He had always hated the prideful thought that hung forever in his mind: my son looks like he's a soldier ready for anything out and about in the world.

The young corporal, just turned twenty years of age, nodded agreement. "I won't sit down in them until I get on the train." He grinned further. "If I skip breakfast, Mom will get upset, so I have no way out of it. They'll get creased up plenty on the train anyway." He sat stiffly at the table. A bright patch of sun, an amber touch of gold alive in it, caressed his hands spread on the table, letting the warm rays bathe the backs of his hands, his wrists, accepting the final comfort of home.

"What time's the train?" Earl said as a portion of morning silence began to eat at him, the kitchen spreading with the sun, yet thinking how the room would diminish in days to come. Perhaps before this day was all the way gone.

The shoulders of his son had widened in the few months since basic training began. Melba, on the other hand, had seen the facial lines develop in her son, the shaving traces, the worry lines, the light shadows in the blond boy's face. The endurance marks, she had called them in her contemplative hours getting ready for bed, shutting down her day. Earl, at counter, had noted the progress of body mass, how the chest deepened, the neck thickened, marking the quick run to manhood. He was no longer the slim defenseman who had little bulk but who had to skate faster than others to stay competitive.

Purly maintained the bright freshness in his face he had always sported. With it he had hidden pain on odd occasions: two broken bones, a collapsed rib or two, and teenage disappointment in the "girlie department," as Earl had called it. "It's running early," Purly said, "real early, collecting other guys on the way here, all the way from Gloucester and Rockport and Ipswich. It'll be here just around 7:30. Six more from here being picked up, Bob Mercer and Chet Russo and Mac Duval, all getting aboard, with some others. Like we're going off on a hockey trip to Canada." He went right to that bright freshness. "Weren't those great days." A heavy laugh rose from his chest, the corporal stripes carried sharper edges, a young man with memories. "I was just thinking about Smitty's father. When I tell that story to some of the guys in the barracks they crack up."

Earl joined the masquerade, his laughter loud and joyous. "That time on the bus?" He had played such games before.

"Oh, yah. How everybody had to keep an eye on him all during the trip, so he wouldn't get caught up in the booze, on his best behavior for a final run. We were all watching him in that last stop in Canada, buying those little nips, then sitting at the back of the bus and getting ready to knock off the first one."

Both of them roared. Earl finished it off, as Purly knew he would. "Tipped that first one and almost drained it off, thinking he had something like Southern Comfort, only Northern Comfort nips were plain maple syrup. 'Member how he almost gagged?"

The two were still laughing when their wife and mother, in full Sunday dress, came into the room.

"What are you two laughing at so early on this morning?" Her whole posture accented her question, her surprise on this last morning. She was dressed for Sunday at church, her hair tied back in a bun. In half an hour she'd have her Sunday hat on her head. The question marked her face, departure of her only son at hand.

Purly got right to the situation. "Mom," he said, "I'd really rather say goodbye here at home, rather than down at the train station in the Center. It'd be a lot easier to cry here."

Earl could never forget the look on Melba's face as she turned to look at her husband, the well-veiled look hidden from her son so that only her husband would know it. "Of course, Purly. You're right. I know I'll cry like a baby and we don't want that."

Earl could easily recall that Purly, even a month younger, could not have said that to his mother. Broader and thicker, he thought, and older.

In a shake of her head she was at the stove, scrambling eggs, bacon cooked beforehand and sitting under a paper towel, coffee aroma hanging in the air. They half joked in talk, a note about where Smitty and his father had gone, what one old girlfriend of Purly's had said one day when Melba was in the market. Melba never mentioned the suffused blush on the girl's face, and never mentioned it to Earl, even in one of her contemplative moods at the side of the bed.

Breakfast, on that harsh morning trying to be casual as ever, was quicker than she wanted, quicker than Earl wanted, but Purly was having his way. He hugged them both in an abrupt moment, grabbed his bag, hugged them again, and strode out the front door and down the street. He looked back a few times, locked them on the porch, turned the corner.

In a minute's time they sped out the back door, Earl going behind the wheel of the old Dodge in a sharp move. Melba closed her door as softly as she could, fearing the echo would rumble down the street, chase her boy around the corner and down Summer Street heading to the center of town, a half mile away.

Earl drove around odd corners, breath heavy in his chest, pulling at unknown parts, scattering in dim places. The knots were there being tied tighter. He tried not to look at Melba, stoic in her seat, and he was thinking that she knew then, at one instant, more than he'd ever know. She was made that way. It was partly why he loved her, the way she noted the noisy board on the porch and that he would never fix it because there was a reason for its being. He felt stupid being stupid, and then clarity hit him bordering on the omnipotent; he too had his values, and the wheel turned in his hands as part of his minor celebration. Past Vinegar Hill he drove, on the far side, and came out behind the fire station. In two more turns she would never have found, he had them three houses down from the railroad station and across the small creek. From the side of friend Greg Satchell's garage they watched Purly and five or six others in uniform board the train and leave home, outbound, bound for war.

They never saw Purly again.

A little over a year later the fire chief started up the front walk, his uniform so crisp it looked brand new, the white hat with dark visor square on his head, and the yellow telegram in one hand. He was the emissary, the arch volunteer, the wound carrier, the harbinger of death, the missing period at the end of a life sentence.

His step was hesitant, his chin stolid and grimly in place, all of it making his uniform crisper, neater, deadlier.

Purly was officially lost in combat in Asia someplace. No country named, no town named, no battle site named. Lost. Missing in action. Just twenty-one, blond and gone forever. When tulips went haywire each May after that, Earl and Melba could put themselves right beside Greg Satchell's little plot of tulips and jonquils, their eyes locked on one figure in uniform. There were days they hated May, days when they waited desperately for the tulips to leap out of bulbs put down in October.

Earl, as personalities continually develop, was the dreamer and Melba the curator of best memories, and owner of tears that Earl had never seen. Earl wrote survival scenarios in his mind, series on top of series of them, plush with dialogue, revelations, possibilities, options, and ultimate survival escapades. Such selections of joy gripped him sometimes for a solid minute of his life, a minute he could carry for an entire day. His thoughts were never clear of them, one or the other hanging by at the back of his head, at immediate bidding.

Now, on this new morning six years later, the war over and never over, his mind at odds, his eyes working extra cautions, his ears like tonal islands except for the most familiar sounds, he saw the shadow in a corner of his eye from a corner of the window. Then he heard the tread on the middle board of the porch.

What? How? He had seen and heard all this before, a hundred times. A hundred times or more. Six years worth of loss and he had seen it all, had heard the same sound, the same shift of weight on one board, and the shade and shape of the shadow now falling into his house again.

Earl Chatsby came up in his chair, erect, mouth open for sound.

He wanted to yell to Melba, but he found no voice. He wanted to believe what he had seen, what he had heard. He wanted to shout, but nothing was down in his throat except an expanse of air. He could not negotiate its passage. It jammed tightly in one place.

When he opened the door to the porch, a blond man stood there, heavy in the face, twisted mustache hanging bars at each corner of his mouth, shoulders not so broad as to mark him. All the scenarios Earl had written for six years fell away, all the survivals, all the hopes, for he had seen this moment coming, but not this man, not this narrow-shouldered man, not this bearer of a wide mustache, not this stranger.

Yet Earl Chatsby also knew he himself had come into a new place, or gone back to an old place.

The man's hands were folded, as in prayer. "Mr. Chatsby," he said in a half voice, as though only half of him was making this visit, "my name is Carl Bollis. It's taken me years to knock at your door." He wrung his hands tighter. "I was with Purly when he died." He started to cry with deep and cumbersome sobs. His body shook. "I always meant to come, but something always held me back." Then another torment broke from him. "It was all my fault. All my fault and he laid down on top of me and took the bullets, took them all."

Earl Chatsby thought the man was going to collapse. All the signs were there. The distinctive ones leaped out: haggard eyes, malnourished face, a man beaten by an awesome enemy without a name as yet. Earl grabbed his arm and ushered him inside. "You have to tell my wife, you have to tell Purly's mother. Please sit down." He thrust him into a chair.

Melba came into the room unprepared for what she saw; a young man who was hungry-looking, malnourished from the first glimpse. Part of the introduction she had heard from the other room. The mother's steps took her back into the kitchen. "Bring him in here, Earl. I'll get him something to eat." She banged about the kitchen as Earl sat their guest at the long kitchen table that he and Purly had built.

"You talk," she said, "and I'll cook. Do you like home fries and sausages and eggs? Don't say no because that's all I have right now." She broke three eggs into a mixing bowl, lit a fire under a frying pan and turned to him. "Please go on."

There followed a long morning between the three, the grieving parents, the grieving comrade, but with minor patchwork changes beginning to incorporate themselves into and about the trio.

Carl Bollis, ever at odds with peace of any kind, at odds with his world for months at a time, felt comfort slowly squeezing around him, like a blanket draping on his body. "I feel Purly here. He talked a lot about this house, about you folks, about hockey trips. I think I know some of your friends, some of his friends. That's hard to say, seeing what I did, what happened back there." A cup of coffee appeared at his hand. One leg stretched out under the table, then the second leg.

Earl and Melba understood Carl Bollis was reaching for something, trying to find a place or a way to a place. Melba placed a full dish in front of Carl, the eggs golden and piled high, the sausages brown as fall, the toast buttered and cut, just the way she set it out for Purly.

Carl Bollis continued. "We were in Burma, part of a special group, specially trained, in great shape. We wanted to do our part. We were ready for it. And Purly was an exceptional soldier. We all knew that from the very beginning. But we were captured by the Japanese because a native betrayed us. We were captives for two years or more. I'm not sure how long, or didn't know then, because everything ran together in the two camps where we were kept prisoners; abuse, pain, hunger, sickness, and more abuse. I won't give any of those details, but Purly always had an idea we could get away, always saying we had to do it by ourselves, not depend on the natives. They were on the sorry end of everything and we couldn't blame them, yet we couldn't trust them. At least, not in the face of torture or worse for their families."

Melba Chatsby, ever-mourning mother, watched the young man talking and eating in her kitchen. Her face gained color, her arms. Something new had become something old, something reaching for her. Air filled her lungs with expectation. Down inside rode a new knowledge. It had become, she suddenly knew, her story. All Earl's scenarios had been related and retold, but now it was her story. She was, in essence, searching for in this stranger a composite trait, a characteristic move that she would recognize in an instant to be what it was, a piece of her son. A composite but nevertheless a piece of her son. Anything was better than nothing. Anything! The fork full of scrambled eggs moved slowly and precipitously to Carl Bollis's mouth, a small chunk falling back on the plate. A speared half link of sausage was chewed only on one side of his mouth. Soon she saw his jaw hanging loose, as if he were enjoying a lingering taste. She looked for Purly, even as the visitor kept talking, kept trying to re-insert her son into her life, right there in her kitchen.

"Purly was working it all the time," Carl Bollis added, "his vision, seeing how we could do it, how many ways and how many pitfalls. But we did it! One night it happened and come morning we were at last five miles from the camp and moving down a stream, three of us. Purly said we couldn't run forever, we'd have to live off the land for perhaps a year, maybe more. We'd have to learn, he said, more than we knew. Stagner got sick and died. We buried him at the back end of a cave, away from animals and the enemy. We were free for a couple of months and were learning. I think Stagner ate something bad or poisonous, because he just rolled over one night sick as hell and was dead by morning. He bloated up terribly."

Earl's mind moved within each descriptive passage delivered by Carl, seeing it all, how Purly moved, how his shoulders were carried by attitude and disposition of the moment, how certain physical motions, precursors or stimuli, were followed by other reflex actions. He remembered all the signatures of his son. And he also saw his wife's intensity filling the room, coming up as wide as life itself.

"We were comfortable, but careful, worried mostly about getting sick. But we had plenty of food. Once we found an aircraft that had crashed in the jungle and we got supplies we hadn't dreamed of. Some medical stuff we wanted desperately. Purly said we were more than a hundred miles by river from Myitkyina, but river travel would seriously expose us. It was the Malikha Stream and would only expose us to the enemy unless we had a target to get to and traveled by night. The odds were against us. Often he talked about waiting out the war, but also laughed at the thought, it was so far out. He had a way of control that was sparkling. He was responsible and he knew it. Smarter than me he was, all the way. We moved away from that place then, worried that the Japanese would find about the plane, or the natives would kick something loose on us. It took us about a week to find another place. We hid from every contact with the natives, afraid to put them at greater risk."

"All the time we watched the skies, and the frequency of our planes. We could feel things changing for the better. Then we were surprised again. They shot at us. I was hit in the leg and the shoulder and fell down. Purly jumped on top of me. They shot at us, straight down at us. Purly took all the bullets. His blood flowed down across my face, flowed into my mouth. I drank his blood. Can you believe that…I drank his blood. I could not cough or gulp and move my eyes. I couldn't blink. I didn't dare blink. The pain was horrible, but I couldn't blink. They kicked us, and laughed and got ready for night."

"Later, one of them, really young, stood over us, his weapon pointing down at us, at me. I swear he was looking at me eye to eye. Firelight was in our eyes, the flames bouncing around. His comrades yelled at him, maybe calling him or ridiculing him. I don't know. They made silly gestures by the fire, as though they were having fun. But he looked hard at me, pointed his rifle and then shot into the ground, right near my face. Right beside my face. I could have been dead. I was thinking all the time, I'll never get away with pretending. Then his buddies began heating water, for making tea I'd guess. I think I could smell it. It was almost totally dark, the fire was bright in the jungle night, and suddenly a plane leaped right out of the sky and strafed us all, killed some of them, scattered the rest. The plane came back and dropped a bomb, and then went on its way. But that soldier, who was my comrade evermore, was killed. The bomb practically dropped right on top of him. I saw him go into pieces. But he was my comrade. Purly was my comrade. If it wasn't for them, I wouldn't be here. Both of them were my comrades. That means forever."

That oath was a fire in his eyes.

He continued his tale, his plate now empty. "In the morning they were gone. I buried Purly under a small tree. All I know is what Purly told me, we were on the Malikha Stream above Myitkyina in Burma. Next day a native boy found me and took me to his village. A runner went off and three days later some of the Marauders came by and brought me to a pick-up point. Later, I was flown out, came home, was discharged after a few months in the hospital, and have worried about this visit every one of my days."

"It's been a bad time of it for me. I've had jobs and lost jobs, maybe dozens of them, but I'm always going back there in my mind, back where Purly is. I have a hard time concentrating. I'm amazed I can tell you all this, mostly because I didn't want to, but I've talked to a lot of guys and they mostly say I owe it to you and Purly. And mostly to Purly at that."

The pause was a long duration. For heavy seconds he turned inward and the kitchen filled with silence floating in air. A heartbeat was heard. A final pronouncement came. "What is not strange is whenever I get a paper cut or nick my finger or bite my lip and try to stop the bleeding, I taste Purly's blood. Without fail," he said. "Without fail."

And there it was for Melba, that absolutely identical tone of his voice, the way his words were finally carried out of his mouth, the way his lips closed down on some words and his eyes cast further explanation. As if he had lost a hockey game and he was at fault. Hockey had never been important to her, but now it was. It was a piece of her son, this sign, his blood having made its move. The sound of Carl Bollis's voice was filling her kitchen with a tell-tale recognition. She heard other sounds; a minor sob, a secret laugh, a last word at the door on the way to school. Whole years rushed at her.

She leaned across the table and looked at him directly. "I figure you may not want what I'm going to say, but you can always hang your hat with us."

Earl stepped in as Carl Bollis stared at his wife. "It's like you brought Purly home with you, Carl. Brought him right back to us from halfway around the world. This is home."

For a fraction of a second Earl Chatsby thought he heard the loose board on the porch give itself away, and a shadow loomed in a corner of his eye.

Apple, for Whom I Have Scoured the Universe

In my hurry
I have scoured
the universe.

She must
be hiding
from me.

Chemkin Albus

While we are here patrolling our lives, moving about, now and then we meet, not with great frequency I must admit, most memorable people. They, in turn, haunt us one way or another until our last vision fades away, be it a turn of their face, a hand's movement in sweet gesture, a universal shoulder announcement as they change direction, or attitude, or deference. Perhaps their impacts are from what they don't do as well as from what they do.

Apple was such a person. She was a highlight marker, bright, nay, brilliant, who was on stage all her life. She knew who she was and where she was going. Often she predicated another's actions, like a cue from the side. I saw it early, yet what a mistake I had made, thinking I was rushing around on my own. All the time, I was being chased.

Now, hanging on a road sign, night worry working its way, trollops in my gut giving out names I can't remember, a single light marks a hillside, and the edge of night sneaking up on me.

The arms of fatigue put forth hands that put forth fingers that touch with foul fervor. I am alone and like it less than last night in a half crowd of other loneliness. The one witness recalled, real as an open blouse, bona fide as underpants dropped the fabulous and witchy length of long and perfect legs, hangs on with her imagery locked in place. Not anything more than one hundred pounds, gymnastically adroit when aboard, mouthing she was performing *the orange squeeze*: I am getting you ready for breakfast, wherever you end up, which will not be on me again, or vice versa. The morning-promised vice went on its rampage, the last ounce ushered into place, heady, sticky later on if only she had left it alone, but oh no, not this imagery aloft in my morning walk who cleaned as good as any kitchen lady at her finishing. Wipe down. Wipe out. How do you like those oranges, my faultless mister in the night?

Now, staring at the next light, the one on the hill known before, the climb to a barn and a gingerly small house that looks down on the sea, the exquisite and lightsome lady there, I bring back the crowded room of smells, liquor on its final legs, dregs at their last cries having found a frame to reside in, sometimes headless, and the little madam of taste that crawled up beside me at the bar, that creature of eyes emblazoned with stories, cheek bones like flint at early manufacture, lips that might stretch a river wide, sex itself having a rest after a heady ride. I'm cheap, she said, a hundred pounds of cheap that two drinks can buy for the night. I liberated myself for a nightly prison. But I'm good at being jailed, being sent off for a one-night stand or a lay-down, or however you'll have it. I never get too talkative. I don't let my mouth get in the way of anything that comes up real. Morning comes too soon, too smelly, too late for some right here, right now. There's not a good piece in this whole joint. All you've got to do is ask me.

You dress well, I said. I touched her fabric and was charged with electrons in a shocking move, a whole laboratory of jump, tingle, and broadcast. Her dress, thin, blue as a forgotten bird's egg, rigged like a sail catching a fresh wind off shore, hip marks saying a vault could be ajar, was right next door to ignition. Right there. Gas-like. Bang! Poof! How do you come across with that heat? Where does it come from? Are shock-proof measures required? Does it have a switch? An off-on switch? A toggle switch? A switch you can see in the dark? Is it universal? Global? A trip around the world? Are you switchable?

Oh, I always need to attract, she said, unfazed, not falsely shocked, not speechless for a single breath, her eyes bouncing, lit. Smallness is too cute for some people, but not taste, those nectars we know. The smile lurked again, a half lip's worth; alliterations do not alienate any matching interests.

Speaking of that, your clothes match well. You are keenly coordinated. What color, or colors if rainbowed, if I may ask, are your underpants? Do they match?

I never wear them, not out here, not out of prison. One drink and I'd put them back on if your thing is getting them off. I've known guys like that, who never get all the way home.Not really. Never really. Too much macho waiting for show. Too much vanity in the way. You know the kind who's afraid to read the sex manuals because he'd know in a fucking second how much he's missed on the way here getting to be forty and near the end. Once I told a guy four or five times he ought to read the good book on sex, and he thought I was ridiculing him or was just playing games, but I was ballicky bare-ass waiting for him to come down where I wanted him desperately and he missed it all. I was lying across the seat of the car and in love I think, my nipples talking to his mouth, saying all the good stuff about attention and how he should be more alert. Only later I found out his wife was hardly the clean type and that foul odor drove him too far afield even of the cleaning lady. I don't know where he went, or if he ever went down, to Australia or any place else, but I hope he's had a good voyage. He was cute too, but even his fingers didn't know what to do, or had not paid attention, never mind his being a good talker. He called me Sam and he loved me, that I know, but could not let go the hard aversions he was trained on. When I touch it all the way every night, it's for him where I left him, on the seat of that old Plymouth convertible parked in a field at the end of a dark lane, a February chill sneaking into the front seat slyer than he was, my Mr. Wanderlust.

Was he not averse to you or something you did or had contemplated? Was it all his fault?

I had intruded on another's family, with the father, and Mr. Wanderlust had his family broken up by the same kind of intrusion. The paired reality hit me but it was only later, after he had gone, that I cemented my own intrusion, getting what I wanted where I wanted it. The revelations do not demand too much explanation; we are what we are. I am the animal mother, the bitch leader, the caller of signals, like the unerring quarterback or like the Pace Car at Indy. I know where I am going and what I am doing, and if you're what I think you are, you won't be far behind me.

One lip curled at my understanding. Oh, yes, I like how your eyes light up at my word play, saying you are alert, that you are in the game.

You read everything at first light, don't you? I like that. There's no bullshit here. I want you on. I want in. I passed my oral exams a long time ago, in the last century.

Her left shoulder moved at further introduction, a breast easing to view, as though it were pure and virginal in its utility, its horizon never at assault, its whiteness further expanding, demanding, commanding, imagination at play, its memory on the move. I contemplated the artful exposure, my mouth stilled with silence, with admiration. Parts of an old story began to unfold, a noun leaked free, a verb, an adverb shook loose in my mind, a mystical story, outworldish, outlandish. Then, oh, fucking loveliness, right then, a fairy of a nipple stood in place, swearing its softness, elfin, impish, exquisite, truly virginal yet truly erect, saying the pot of gold was at hand. My little one-hundred-pounder, without underpants in place, sliding effortlessly on eggshell blue silk, everything moving in place, replied: You're like the wide-eyed kid in the front row at school, the one who sucks up everything that comes his way, who gets an *A* in every exam and every test and every dinky quiz thrown at him except how to get out of the classroom if there is a fire. Do I read that you have missed something here? Are you not my Mr. Wanderlust come back again?

You mean, from that old Plymouth convertible, where you had shared another man with another woman?

That old altar is yet in place, locked away for the evermore, the sense of urgency that drove me there, undressed me, put me prone and lascivious, hangs about dense as a dream nearly gone over the edge, but never letting go. Always, the night temperature of that far field of that dark lane touches with its long reach, the way it slipped in through the canvas top, came up through the fabric of the seat, set my sweet little ass on fire. Oh, the subtle ironies that impale me.

I'll meet you in the barn.

We went home, by different routes, to the house on the hill, the single light still lit, the mow in the barn piled high with fresh hay, me and my salty actress.

On the way up a single leaf shone with a ray of universal light. She was never far afield no matter what old Chemkin said. I had found Apple's orchard.

Strangers to Love

I won't coerce you. You can believe what you want about things that happened back in 1944, in that *other* century, but Willie Kriegslin, of course, never existed, never made love more than a dozen times in a secret cave in Maine with a seventeen-year-old farmer's daughter whose name was Emsie Felton, never escaped from the POW camp near Houlton, never served with minor distinction in the 90th Light Afrika Division of the German Afrika Corps in the Sahara Desert during World War II, never contemplated murder or marriage. You can believe all that if you want. But I wouldn't. Take it from me.

All that said, love *was* afoot.

In the dead of silence it happened, at the hour before the false dawn, the sky still bristling with stars, a low moon heating memories, when a voice from outside echoed through the cave. For the third time of this late night encounter, Emsie had borne Willie's weight, fearful each coupling might be the last, her grasp telling him so—and the deep rhythm coursing down through flesh and bone, running with her blood. It made way in her fingertips, in the newly-remarkable span of her thighs, in that place where her heart might have been, now knocked asunder and beating fitfully. Movies had done this to her, and stage plays, and everyday drama crawling through or exploding on those otherwise common days, all exposed to her by her mother who could have been imprisoned by the farm and its insistent, laborious demands. But wasn't. Nor would her daughter be so shackled.

And the young German prisoner helped with his part.

With Willie there were moments, such as at this interruption, when Emsie thought not a breath was left in her lungs, the way wind left her, with a rushing noise and added expectation, like parts of an orchestra coming and going, the brass horns ringing, the violins lingering. Willie had accomplished that from the first encounter. And all of it now erupting simultaneously behind her eyeballs, seeing things that did not exist, not as yet, images of the future carved by her mind and frozen in place, just when the harsh voice rocked through the cave on the far edge of the Felton farm. The voice was raucous and metallic and she immediately recalled a *King Lear* play in Boston and a stagehand, a musical stagehand she supposed, for battle and storm presentation beating a large sheet metal plate, hanging from the rafters, with a huge rubber mallet. In row three, at her mother's treat, she had shivered away any disbelief of the spectacle.

This night of the cave was in late August of 1944. The invasion of Europe had begun two months earlier, with measurable noise and thrust, on the coast of France, the German campaign in Africa having been shut down fifteen months earlier, and the world going topsy-turvy once again. Most of the potato crop had been picked and packed off and cellar barrels in many parts of Maine stacked with taters and salted cod. A minor chill slipped in from the northwest sly as an infiltrator, winter's hello fully presumed, its signs known quietly. The days, one at a time, came differently, making announcements on their own selection, nature assisting, demands being made. A few of them were subtle for starters, as high-based color turned with a slow, tempered ignition. Early daylight sky behind familiar silhouettes became, by degrees, a hard blue, stark and clean-edged, as if cut deeply into cerulean ice. And pinnacled. Singular pine trees, at a glance, stretched the Earth for all it was worth, lifting selves mightily. Mountains appeared proud as a woman's morning breasts matching her hipline, blankets astray on the far side of sleep, night tossed aside, messages rampant and understood.

Only Emsie and her brother, now in California, had known about the cave on the edge of the family farm. Nobody else had ever visited there, she was sure. But Willie had found it, all as if she had been waiting for such discovery, and such a man with such a way.

The cave, hidden by the tangle of old trees, was on the side of a hilly ledge, and tipped slightly downward toward the entrance, providing quick release for rain or ground water. This made the cave habitable though small, and good for drying out, for secrets, for love making its way at the edge of Willie's escape. Granite reaches seemed spawned from the cave itself, great slabs this end of the earth openly wore as signatures of another era. The cave, calved by a glacier instead of by fire in an earlier millennium, had been formed out of huge slabs, but was no longer a significantly cool place. Graffiti, a long way off, had not touched it yet, though minor fires later on had, sheets of smoke leaving a texture of smudges, burnt spots, darkened fingerprints. In other caves a world away, Pre-Adamites or Paleolithic people, perhaps, had lingered, drawn wall relics, and passed on, leaving their best interests. Willie had managed a visit to a cave discovered in 1940 in Lascaux, southwest France, before his assignment to the German Afrika Corps in the Sahara. He was an amateur spelunker and Emsie believed he was born for this cave, though few people knew about it, probably including those Pre-Adamites or Paleolithic peoples. Pure fate was on her side.

But now, before the dawn flash, someone else did know: Elwood Felton, the owner of the threatening, baritone voice.

"Whomsoever's in that damned hole better get their ass out of there right now else I'll fill it with enough buckshot to make 'em a decent burial." His voice was louder than any Panzer sergeant's and Willie Kriegslin stiffened in place.

Felton's daughter, Emsie, not quite bordering on lovely, dreamy but spontaneous, thrill still random in her, quickly draped her hand over Willie's mouth. "Don't say anything, Willie. That's my father. I'll go. If he beats me, don't hurt him, promise me that. Don't try to kill like you did in the desert. I remember what you said about Gazala and Tobruk and El Alamein. How you were captured. I know you're glad it's over. We're both out of the war now. Promise not to hurt him. He doesn't know any better."

At those words Willie's right hand was cupping Emsie's breast, her elegance and forgiveness encapsulating him. His English was imperfect, but she could understand him, piece it together with apparent ease, smile continuously, touch back. He said, "No officer ever told me I'd meet a girl like you. I am filled. I do not want to release the riches in my hand. But that voice out there is more than a threat. It tells me I might never touch you again. God forbid that, no, not ever again." Such thoughts rushed him quicker than any image of the prison camp and what was promised him anew because of this aborted escape. "Never have I known this kind of sweetness. The softness you bear. What magic passes into me from a mere girl with arctic blue eyes and dimpled cheeks and artistic hands. Whose flanks swallow me truly."

She shivered again and deepness resounded in him for the first time in his life, a bell ringing for all it was worth, pushing at his skin as if it were to break through and shatter him. "Oh, Emsie, pieces of my soul are being cut to pieces. If I were to die, I swear I'd never let go." But Emsie, even at hearing her father's voice and ever at control, guided his hands in a last pass at mystery, to that near elsewhere where other matters had already concluded.

"Whatever happens, Willie, don't you forget me. Don't you dare. Not ever."

They had enjoyed two weeks of being lovers, two weeks of tempest and tribulation, two weeks of discovery, the old and the new. She had been told everything. Willie had escaped from the POW camp when he followed, at a discreet distance, a Kommando officer who had fooled the Americans into thinking he was only a dumb foot soldier. All through his young war, Willie had been led by such men. For the early years in the army the future was always with the man leading him in battle. Supposedly, that future had changed.

When Emsie's father yelled at the mouth of the cave, darkness had molded everything but Willie's hand. There, that elegance of the lingering breast kept shivering back at him, the messages lasting until that precise moment. A ball of breath, in his chest, held its place, the hunger frozen in form, swearing to last forever. He kissed her one last time and saw the whole movie developing right in front of his eyes. It was all black and white and ran quickly, in a newsreel fashion, with scenes leaping place to place.

Emsie, in her own rush at recapture, saw again the flash of her own recent history, her angled views of Willie Kriegslin from the first moment he had dropped off the tail end of the army truck weeks earlier in her father's yard. She felt all the righteous signals the moment her eyes drew level to this young prisoner brought to the farm on the large truck, along with other German prisoners, to bring in the potato crop. All the commanding parts of her body had been screaming for something like this for months on end. The other parts did not count. Reality, at length, stood on its hind legs, breathed, moved as graciously as a dancer, understood what was about him. This handsome blond with the wide shoulders began to play the rhythms in her bloodstream. Announcements leaped out of her. She saw where they landed, down in the fishing hole depths of his eyes where something frolicked, counted hours, played back a chorus of answers no other soul in the universe was privy to. Knowledge leaped upon her, found its way home to belief.

The prisoners had climbed down from the tail end of the six-by truck, mostly looking like roustabouts from fairs or carnivals. And there stood blond and wide-shouldered Willie Kriegslin, young POW, starkly blue-eyed and yet somehow innocent in what mild measurement she could muster, it being enough for her. The only place of comfort for her in this whole terrible world, now hurling pieces of hot metal at each other from one end of the planet to the next, was contemplating a handsome German war prisoner, looking lost in the depths of Maine. A handsome boy, indeed, extracted from the hell of his war.

Her heart leaped, a bit in sympathy, a bit in lust, a bit of curiosity riding her for the next few days.

The wide shoulders had come first to her, the near unreal span of them compared to what was left of the young male population in town, all the others called to war, and his eyes so much like the eyes she had last seen on her Golden Lab with his collar hooked on a tree being driven in the rush of the Allagash River's white waters, a look she would never forget. As Emsie might have said to anybody who'd listen to her, she was ready for Willie who, obvious to her, was appointed at this time to come into her life, safely and wholly extracted from the war.

And Elwood Felton, scene stealer, yelled again; "I ain't gonna say it again, mister. Git'n your ass outta there is the best part of advice you can expect, 'cause there ain't gonna be no more." Buckshot came from the shotgun burst off a rock outside the cave, and the noisy blast bounced into the cave, ricocheting off granite surfaces worn smooth by a hundred millenniums. "I knowed you was in there last night. I just waited up for day comin'."

Emsie whispered in Willie's ear, "We're not done yet, Willie. I'll see that true." She moved against his hand, and then guided it in a last touch. "You remember me, Willie, no matter how long it takes. You remember me."

Rolling away from her lover, she sat up and yelled out. "Don't shoot any more, Pa. I'm coming out. Willie and I are friends." She could have sung those words, but her father would certainly be tone deaf to their meaning.

When Willie Kriegslin followed Jaeger Brecht out of the POW camp at Houlton, by less than a half hour, he was, for all his intents, the dumbest of the POWs in the camp. The main thing Willie had in his favor was he knew who Jaeger Brecht was, the Kommando colonel in masquerade, who had completely fooled his American captors into believing he was nothing but another dumb soldier, unaware of the big picture. Brecht was the ace up Willie's sleeve.

Brecht had no idea Willie was following him and had generally ignored the comrade who openly admitted, to anyone who was listening, that he was just a dog soldier, a foot slogger only obeying directions of his officers. Back in Edenkoben in the Rhineland, Willie's father was a mere cobbler, struggling in that small town, living veritably from foot to mouth. Willie, at an early age, knew he was destined for the same task; the only other choice was to break out and work in the vineyards. Oftentimes looking at his future, he fostered a joy in hunting and fishing and was comfortable in the forests and in mysterious caves and by the water. All these provided escape for him, never dreaming of being a soldier, until the army pulled him into the ranks. From then on he followed where he was pointed. Now, at a distance, in all the stealth imaginable, he had followed the Kommando officer, who had carefully planned every step of his escape from the POW camp, through the broken fence, the twisted wires, the open culvert under the last barrier.

All Willie carried with him was a batch of pepper wrapped in a handkerchief and carried in a paper bag. During his potato picking that August, on various farms in the Houlton area, Willie had found the hidden cave at the edge of the Felton place, and had stashed stolen supplies during a month of odd labor, potato picking and daily intrigue. First he placed water in odd containers in the cave, and scrounged food from farmer's wives or daughters, that would last at least a week, perhaps time enough for any concentrated pursuit to slacken. One old map of the state of Maine came into his hands at the back of a barn, and that too rested in the cave.

The pepper was for the dogs that would follow them. He had seen Brecht for weeks take away from meals every bit of pepper he could manage. And Willie followed suit, knowing what the pepper was for. Let the dogs come; all he had to do was to get to the cave, live on his stored supplies, move on later when the pepper did the trick on the dogs, the chase cooled, and the Americans went back to their laid-back ways.

During the escape he dwelled at times on the daughter at the Felton farm who smiled at him once or twice, as if a message was being sent. Emsie was one of prettiest girls he'd seen in America, and she had a good shape, worked hard and was only seventeen. He admired all that in her, and her smile. It was evident to him very early that she turned her back when he was busy at secret things, as if she was eager to help him, or at least averting her eyes; she'd not be a good witness if he fled. With no young men on the farm, Willie was sure he was attractive to her, as she was attracted to him. He began to think about her in that way. Once, when he went into the barn and stayed there for ten minutes, she had casually walked in and began to talk to him. Willie's English was good enough to be understood, and his leanings for her were clearly pronounced. When she stood close enough for him to kiss her, as if daring him, he did. Her arms wrapped about him and she pressed herself against him. "Willie," she said, "you are the strongest one ever to work here. I like that. I like you, but we have to be careful. My father would beat me if he saw me. He wouldn't understand. He never does."

"You make me dream about you," Willie said, as he hugged her tightly. "I dream about you every night back at the camp. When can I be with you? I do not want you to get into any trouble, because I am meaning to escape from the camp and hide out in the woods. The camp is a horrible place. No privacy. No women, no *you*, it makes everybody crazy, the way simple things go out of kilter. Things go unbalanced. It happens every day. The men are remembering wives or sweethearts. I have nobody but you to think about. I can be crazy for you, but I don't want you to get in trouble, you work so hard and so good. You work as hard as any man I've ever seen, but you always look better than any of them to me."

There was no argument that she'd be in good hands with Willie Kriegslin. The thought went through her sure as a vow, and as solid. This early in life, she had found her man. Revelations come to the young too, she thought. And she swore she could see the future, could touch it, taste it, bring it to bed with her every night. She hugged him again, in the barn, out of sight of the entire universe itself. She also swore the yellow-green eyes of two horses in separate stalls were looking at her sadly.

In the cave, dark as any night cell and no hope for starlight, Willie imagined what lurked around him. He conjured up a vast array of shapes and shadows in the corners of his eyes.

The odd apparitions of youth came back with their opaque being; he saw things that were not there. Emsie, of course, began her intrusions, three nights in a row assailing him with her trim body, the smell of her skin even in the field under the sun. He would know her any place, could smell her on the thinnest sheet of air. It was the third night, the farm quiet, no stars because of cloud cover; that Willie dared to think about leaving the cave. The little bag of pepper, which had come in so handy with the dogs in chase, was as good as a weapon. He kept it in a pocket of his pants, and could smell the aroma once in a while. As he was making a decision to at least get some exercise, he heard the first odd noise, first of rock against rock, slight, secretive, then a rustle of clothes, and a small waft of air came against his face and he smelled Emsie, knew she was entering the cave, with the first sound had moved the rock at the entrance.

"Willie," she said, "it's me, Emsie. I'm coming in." Now he could really hear the rustle of her clothes and he caught her scent on a small draft of air, as if she had sent it on to him, to tease him or find acceptance.

"I know you've been hiding here. I'm the only one who knows this place, besides my brother, and he's in California now, working on planes. Even my father doesn't know. He'd skin me alive if he knew I was in here. Would have done it years ago, too. So we never told him. I haven't been in here since my brother Jimmy left. He had to go. My father treated him like a disaster, kept after him forever. Jimmy was never going to be like him. I'm staying, have stayed for my mother or I would have followed Jimmy to the West Coast. I could be making planes that are fighting your army, your friends. I hate war. It's so cruel. We should all be friends, but I'm afraid we can't be friends with Hitler. Even some of your own army officers tried to kill him. Why did they do that?"

"Can you stay with me?"

"Only until 3 in the morning or about then. He's always up by five; hard work is all he knows."

"Do you want to stay?"

"That's why I came." I've been dreaming about you. Like every night. I don't think of you as an enemy. I can't explain it all, but I had to come. I knew you were here the first night, but I didn't want you to get caught. There have been soldiers everywhere, even dogs sniffing around, but they didn't come near this cave. They went on past the end of the wall and into the woods at the end of the field."

She was in his arms and her essence assailed him. It was as if she was all exposed with her clothes still on.

"Last warnin', to the pair of ya. Git out'n here now 'fore I let loose. Emsie, you come first, girl. I ain't meanin' to shoot ya, but I sure am itchin' with this trigger."

"Pa, we're coming together. Don't dare shoot. I'm not letting go of him. I love him, Pa, I don't care if he is a German. He's the man I want to marry some day."

"And let me be the laughin' stock of the whole town? Not on your bottom dollar."

"You use their muscle to get your potatoes, and you'll spend the earnings, but you won't listen to what fits me."

Emsie came out first, as she pulled Willie along behind her coming out of the cave. She stood up shielding Willie, directly in front of the shotgun. "I love him, Pa. Don't make any mistake about that. I've spent near a week with him, right here. Don't spoil anything, Pa."

Her father, taking one hand off the gun, slapped her hard on the face. Willie leaped at him. The shotgun went off and Willie, wounded for the first time since entering the army, screamed in pain. He fell to the ground. Emsie screamed at her father and then pulled the gun out of his hands. He had never shot a man before.

Shouts came from back at the farmhouse and barn. Dogs barked. An engine, loud in the pre-dawn, roared down on them from the service road.

Soldiers came. They put Willie in the back of the truck. Emsie kissed him goodbye as three soldiers laughed at her. "He's the goods, is he? Nothing but a Kraut. Ya ought to know better. They'll take care of him now, probably knock a rape charge against him." The talker, a sergeant, looked at Emsie's father. "How's that sit with you, sir, a rape charge. We'll make it tight. Make it stick. Me and these others practically came right up on them, him, in the act. In a dark cave to boot. Be a piece of cake making it stick. It might be a little easier for you around here, knowing what the neighbors'll make of all this, a loose farm girl you know."

"Go to hell with your rape charge," said Emsie, "and your noise about a loose farm girl. I'll bet you weren't so lucky, not around here anyway. I love him. He's going to be my husband some day when the war is over." For one bare moment, she was an historian looking down the road in front of her. "All wars get over, and friends get made up again. You'll see." She stared at Willie leaning out of the back of the truck. "Willie, I'll love you all the way until this war gets over. You remember where I am. I'll be here. If they try to charge you with rape, I'll go to the newspapers myself, or I'll go down to the camp and make hell for them. You're going to be my husband someday."

"Not goin' to be no husband, not on my farm, he ain't," her father said.

The sergeant added his own forecast, "We'll ship him so far from here, he'll never find his way back. Does that suit you, sir? That make it up to you for what's happened here?" Emsie remembered the sergeant was the one who had twisted Willie's arm half up his backside when he shoved him into the truck, with pleasure riding his smile, and knew his face would forever be at call. At that moment she also realized that he would share space with Willie in her mind. It reinforced a belief she held that love could often be unfair.

Resolute, a small storm riding her backside, anger making way its entry, Emsie turned her back on the sergeant, and leveled a broadside at her father. "Then, I'll just have to go off like my brother did, driven off to the other side of the country just because he didn't see things the way you did." Her father saw his daughter at that instant as solid as the rocks about them.

She turned to her new friend and lover, hope more alive on her face than ever before, eyes vibrant and reaching, casting a sense of ownership, and yet accompanied by an oath in her words. That's when Elwood Felton saw the second materialization of his wife for the first time in years, when Emsie said, "If I ain't here when you come back, Willie, I'll be in Orinda, California with my brother Jimmy. Jimmy Felton, Orinda, California, so far from here nobody else can get there but you, and nobody else wanted there but you." She nodded at the sergeant, "Let this man make a liar out of the truth and see where it gets him before I get done with all this."

She threw Willie a kiss.

In the pale remnants of early morning she was an upright sign of the new day, and over one shoulder, as if called on for dual announcement, the dawn flash leaped up over a crowned hill and stressed her singularity. Emsie Felton was, without sergeant stripes or parental authority, in charge of the future looming in front of them, and the escaped and recaptured German prisoner of war, staring at her over the tailgate of a six-by army truck, believed he was seeing life already unfolding for him from where it had been sent off by another smaller god of the universe. He had met so few of them.

Swan River Daisy

C hester McNaughton Connaughton, aptly named for both sides of the family, landowner in the new world, squeezer of pennies and nickels at the very corpulence of coin, embarrassed at times by his own good fortune where his roots had once been controlled and ordained by potatoes and turnips or the lack thereof, gazed over the latest acquisition of a two-acre parcel abutting his prime abode and wondered how he could best utilize it. Mere coinage, he had early assessed, would apply the jimmy bar under Carlton Smithers and separate him from the land in their town of Saxon. Carlton was old, alone, susceptible. It would be a piece of cake. It was, subsequently and as he had forecast, a swift steal, and papers and proper process moved the property under the shield of his name.

A big man in his own right, massive across the shoulders, Chester, even as a dreamer of large proportions, was given to talking to his father long gone down the pike, from a runaway case of pneumonia, to better pasture. The old gent had once called it *a greater kingdom and a lesser court*. Still civil in such matters, Chester addressed his father as "sir," never once forgetting his manner of address. "Sir," he said this day, "how can I best use this land? The farmer is no longer in me, no endless hours, no thievery of land and what it will allow to be taken from it, these I do not envision. What would you propose? I would by design do whatever you suggest." On his porch, the sun pushing its heat across the width of the two acres, Chester transposed himself into his study mode.

Now it takes all kinds of beliefs to manage oneself in this world, and commerce or business demands certain of those beliefs come into the fate of a man. Chester heard his father say, in the same enigmatic voice, the same wonder of voice, the simple words, *Swan River Daisy*, the words a barely audible breath coming upon his porch, like an aside from forever. The long-gone old man had not entirely eluded him. A sense of trust redoubled itself in him as he heard the echo say again, from some parallax athwart the universe, *Swan River Daisy*, and repeating, *Swan River Daisy*.

Acceptance struck him. Oh, he knew that sun-yellow flower well, a hardy, deep-root grower that dispelled an easy pull of root work in the fall. One year a decade or so earlier he had planted the whole flower bed across the front of the old colonial house with the tenacious daisies, waiting for their yellow waves to unfold a day in May, a wave a teasing breath of wind could set to dancing, the daisies standing so tall. Both the blossoming and the root work came back to him in swift recall. Did the old man mean to have him construct a greenhouse on the property, to specialize in Swan River Daisies? Was that the evolution of the simple answer a soft wind had brought him across the field? Should he plant the whole field with such golden color it would attract tourists? Should he run horses, like roans and pintos, through the field, and to what end? What good means is such advice without fair and equitable interpretation?

At length, in this quandary, the sun nodded his head and closed his eyes, and the old man said again from off the porch yet at immeasurable distance, *Swan River Daisy.*

Came upon him eventually turmoil and noise and his daughter crying out to him, "Father! Father! Look, look at the field!"

Upon his new property sat the most gorgeous Mississippi paddle wheel steamboat he had ever seen. It was red and blue of color and proud in its bearing and was smoking at its single black stack. Bales of cotton, like pale brown dominoes, stood on the prow of its deck and the paddle wheel astern of it, like a huge radius, spun itself through slow, angry revolutions. But there were no passengers crowding its deck, no crew evident about its surfaces, no movement other than smoke in a single column drifting upward to dispersion and the paddle wheel only partly visible in its circular passage.

Boldly printed in large yellow letters against the blue hull was the name, "Swan River Daisy."

In less than the passage of one hour he was nearly assaulted by the building inspector who had come in answer to neighbors' complaints, his eyes popping, his hands in agitated gesture. "How did you get it here? Did you have a permit? Do you have a permit? Was there a building plan submitted to Town Hall before this traffic? I suspect, sir, that you have violated many laws and regulations and will be held accountable."

Chester shrugged his shoulders. "I did not bring it here. How could I do that? It was just there. My daughter, in great confusion, yelled at me and said, 'Look in the field.' There it was."

"Is that your field?" The inspector was indeed young, indeed officious and surly in manner, the way Chester looked upon him, and wore his hair long and uncombed.

"Yes, I bought it quite recently." A pup is still a pup, Chester announced to himself.

"I suggest, sir, that this must go all the way to the mayor. You, most likely, as I have said, have broken all kinds of rules. That plot is not zoned for business." The inspector was young, snotty-nosed, arrogant in an imperial and puerile manner at one and the same time, and was shaking his head and pointing the most possible accusatory finger at landowner Chester McNaughton Connaughton, smarting at the surliness.

"What business is that, inspector? Chester could not bring himself to call the young man *sir*. That was reserved for his father. His father came from that distant point again, that far parallax, *Swan River Daisy.*

The wide-eyed young inspector, obviously not in on the other conversation, replied, from his haughty countenance, "Why, that of transportation, having a river boat, delivering cotton bales, obviously a horde of passengers who are below deck and gambling illegally." His head shook in a fearfully authoritative manner, superior counsel judging the Swan River Daisy from his dais, and thus judging Chester McNaughton Connaughton.

"Delivering bales where?" Chester's hands were on his hips, his arms like sails, a big man towering over the young judge in pants though not in robe.

"Why, the next port of call, perhaps." The young man looked down past the fields the way one might look down river. Fluster, for the lack of another expression, came on him. "I must report this to higher authorities. I will call the electric and telephone and cable companies to see if any of their wires have been cut or disturbed. This is highly unusual. Improper displacement of utilities most certainly has been commissioned in this transport. Think of all your neighbors so unceremoniously impacted. Perhaps half the town. Why haven't I been so informed?" In the most inquisitive gesture, he cocked his head to one side, a half smile at his mouth, as if to say *you can let me in on this*, and said, "How did you ever in this world navigate the underpass from the main highway? That seems quite impossible."

"I suspect it does look that way, but I did not bring it here. I did not build it. I did not order it. I did not wish for it. And I assure you I know nothing about the underpass or the overpass or how it was, as you say, navigated." Chester suspected there was in his own eyes a merry twinkle at this point. He consciously depressed the words, "Perhaps there's been a change of tide."

"But, sure as heaven, you are responsible for it." The finger was wagging at Chester once more. "It's on your property, sir, and you are therefore responsible. I hope you have insurance."

"For what?" replied Chester, still hearing the far voice saying, "*Swan River Daisy.*"

"For the obvious damages you have incurred getting it here."

"Getting what here?"

"Getting the Swan River Daisy onto your property, that's what. I can read the name on the hull. I know what a Mississippi steamboat is, and a stern paddle wheeler for all that. You can't fool me in these matters. I assure you I have read *The Adventures of Tom Sawyer*. I know about the big river and the boats. I even saw the movie, Tom and Huck and Becky in the cave. And Injun Joe." A pause came upon the young inspector, jaw hanging slack, then a distant light came into his eyes as he stuttered in saying while pointing at the Swan River Daisy, "This… this, sir… this is not Saxonish. This is," and he held his breath in proper caesura before he nearly shouted out, "Mississippian." As he walked away, Chester McNaughton Connaughton saw a definite slump had accosted the young man's shoulders.

In less than another hour a parade of men and two women came to Chester McNaughton Connaughton as he and his daughter Chadra were leaning on the fence that girded the new parcel of land, and the Swan River Daisy was still puffing a thin line of black smoke, the wheel still turning mysteriously into the earth, and as yet no passengers or crew were evident. Counted in that new audience were the mayor, the town counsel, three men from the Planning Board and two women dressed in rose-colored dresses, an energetic member of the Appeals Board who was rapidly making notations on a pad of paper, and citing the length of the Swan River Daisy by use of a visimeter of a special sort. Every man was dressed in a black suit, white shirt and black tie and Chester, whispering to his daughter, said, "They look like hangmen if you ask me." To which the daughter replied, "Especially the women in those deep-rose dresses, so ghastly."

The mayor, bristling, holding forth in front of the small parade, addressed Chester McNaughton Connaughton. "My dear Mr. Connaughton, what is going on here?" With his hands on his hips he was still half the size of Chester, yet he had a round face, almost moonlike above the black tie, and deeply set eyes continuously at measurement. "This disturbance, this disdain. I was at a wedding reception. It is no mean fete to slip away from a wedding reception. I'll have you know. I might have dishonored a constituent."

Chester reminded himself of the change of tide comment and

thought well of it. "Do you seek passage, sir? Do you sail? Indeed, I do not, and do not contemplate doing so."

"Is this your craft?" the mayor, whose name was Anton Mustain, said to Chester, and then smiled at the two ladies from the Appeals Board. He did not know which one he favored best.

"It is not my craft. It is not my boat. It is not my ship."

"Is this your land?"

"We all know this is my land," Chester offered, leaning back against the split rail fence. "I bought it from Carlton Smithers."

The mayor smirked for the ladies once more. "At a ridiculously low price, from what I hear."

"Would you have bought it at that price?" Chester said.

"That's beside the point," the Mayor said.

"Precisely what I say," Chester came back with. "It's all beside the point. This is not my paddle wheeler."

"If it stays here in your field, you will have to pay taxes." In his affirmation, Anton Mustain was holding the hand of one of the ladies of the Board of Selectmen. He squeezed that hand as a sign of his authority and their potential. "That means property taxes, water fees, sewerage fees, all that apply to a place of business. The Assessors are at this moment coming up with a firm billing." He felt puffed and thorough and mightily superior.

"To what business do you refer?" Chester said.

"The business of commerce, sir. It is most evident that this craft is a business enterprise. My god, man, look at the piles of cotton bales on the prow of that craft."

"Do you suggest that I have a cotton field where such cotton is raised?"

"Where you get it, sir, is your concern. Mine is that you pay the appropriate fees for running such a business."

"If I offered you for the taking every bale of cotton, would you take them, for free?" Chester offered. Chadra Connaughton squeezed her father's hand.

"What in heaven's name would I do with bales of cotton? Where would I take them?"

"Your Building Inspector, whom I note did not return with you, suggested the next port of call, down river somewhere."

"My god, sir, there is no river here."

"That is precisely my argument, Mr. Mayor. There is no river to properly run a business of boats. There is no next port of call. There is no place to deliver the goods of a business. There is nothing. This town has not supplied any services for such a business. And you wish to tax me on those conditions."

"By god, sir, there is a boat in your field and you will pay taxes on it." His voice was a few octaves up on its normal range. The lady of the held hand squeezed him back. He turned to the assessor still madly scribbling on his pad. "I want the whole business of this land sale scrutinized before this day is out. We will get to the root cause for all actions, mark my words. And once you have ascertained the proper tax billing, please present it to Mr. Connaughton." He squeezed the lady's hand and said, in his best manner, "And with a duplicate copy to me so that I can fully watch and control this situation myself, if I must say so."

The parade of authority of the town of Saxon walked off behind the mayor, who strutted like a drum major at the head of a band.

Chadra Connaughton tugged her anxiety at her father's sleeve. "Easy, child," he said, "it will be fine with us. We have done no wrong."

When Mayor Anton Mustain woke in the morning and looked out his back window, hoping to catch the glint of the early sunrise, the Swan River Daisy, on due course, was now crowding his whole back yard.

The Cochran Resolve

C losing on forty-five years on the Saugus Police Department, all of it on the street it seemed except for the last few years of count-down to his retirement, Silas Tully owned up to a few things. If he were asked to give a thumbnail sketch of himself he would have replied simply, but very graphically, as follows: God-fearing, American to the absolute and final core, stiff believer in the Marine Corps and its heady history, a cop every day until his last day, and a detailer. That he loved, and lived by, details, was a paramount importance in all he did. So it was not odd that in 1990, late in the year, leaves crisp and yellow as butter or red as lava flow, the stadium a full bandbox of sounds on Saturdays, dates and anniversaries and common events came piling across the back of his mind like some inner movie being run for the hundredth time.

Silas Tully always paid heed to such home movies. Now the old headlines grabbed at him, tossed their thick and tall blackness and page-wide shrieks into his mind, their gripping attention reaching out to him. *MURDER* they had screamed, *VIOLENT MURDER, a girl, a nice neighborhood girl, some fifty years ago, garroted and strangled and fiercely and barbarously treated and then dumped off the side of a lonely road.*

He'd been just a spanking brand new fifteen-year-old when the murder had taken place, and even now, after all the years on the force, after all he had seen and wished he hadn't seen at times, the newer murders, the later crimes, the heinous deeds he had been sometimes witness to, it still came at him as if it had happened only yesterday.

It had happened almost fifty years ago, and Silas Tully found an old reproduction of a *Lynn Daily Evening Item*, one he had finally Xeroxed before it gave up the ghost, the Cream of Wheat texture of it, the aging yellowness falling away to near dust. He read again the lead paragraph, a paragraph some reporter had written when Silas was a mere fifteen years old, a paragraph hard enough to make any man sit up, even today: *Twenty-four hours after the mutilated body of attractive Frances Cochran, nineteen-year-old bookkeeper, of 54 Water Street, was found in a thicket near the Salem-Lynn-Swampscott line police were seeking the driver of a '34 or '35 Chevie with yellow trimmings.* The Chief of Police had reported that a mysterious caller to a local radio station had advised that a body could be found off Danvers Road. Frances Cochran had disappeared on July 17 and was the object of an intense search for three days before her body was discovered. After the tipster called, two Swampscott patrolmen had found her body.

Silas Tully could still feel the taste in his mouth, all these years later, which the story had induced. He found nothing as despicable as hurting the fair sex, and knew that much of his character and all of his police life had been painted by that distaste. Now and then he shook in anger at such doings. It made him work much harder than the guy next to him.

The girl's body was found with her face and head bludgeoned into a pulp, her skull crushed and parts of her shoulders and torso burned in a crude attempt to burn the body. Her teeth were broken and her entire body maltreated. Her clothing was torn to shreds. "Absolute barbarism and the work of a crazed fiend or a maniac," said the chief. A tree twig, about an inch in thickness, was found lodged deeply in Miss Cochran's throat. The body was sprawled in a tangle of brush about thirty-five feet from the road.

The beastliness of it all came full charge at him, a horrible sense of the deed working on him as strong as it had when he was that

mere boy. Over and over again he read the story, assimilating every
detail, categorizing and filing each little item, each entity or bit of
information, and slowly and surely, the way a glacier makes its
way out of the mountains, a matter of resolve began to fill him.
From every known source he gathered additional details, taking
Xeroxes of everything in the files of *The Lynn Daily Evening
Item* and *The Salem Evening News.* In turn he was lead on to
clippings from a number of Boston papers, the *Globe* and the
Herald and *Traveler* and the *Record and American* and the old
Post, and subsequently to an innumerable number of magazine
articles and specialty features on one of the most brutal of crimes.
Certainly, for those along the North Shore, from tightly packed
Winthrop under the sound of aircraft popping in and out of
Boston's Logan Airport to the water-world that was Gloucester
and Rockport and Manchester-by-the-Sea, the crime was one for
the century.

And for the fact that half of that century was about to pass,
Officer Silas Tully, God-fearing, American, Corps' man, cop
forever, detailer (*Ars Punctilio*, as Chief Noel Rebenkern had so
often referred to him), sitting daily now in the soft chair easing
him down the road to retirement, decided to have a go at it himself!

The chief wondered what the hell was keeping Silas so busy,
reading and poring over notes and literature, copying newspaper
and magazine clippings, burning both ends of the candle with
retirement just over the hill. But he knew his man as well as any
man, and if this bulldog of a cop had got his bite onto something,
then someone someplace or somewhere should be wary. In his
own way he pictured Si a long time in the past working behind the
Japanese lines a mere two hundred yards off the beach of some
now-quieted but memorable Pacific island. It could make the most
alert man nervous.

"Si,' he said, one day late in October, coming into work and
the crisp air of the outside a cool and vivid memory on his face as
he passed by Silas, "What the hell's got you perked up? You've
been poring over that material for a week now." He hitched his

belt up and pulled at it, as if to redistribute his bodily matter and to make himself taller, the textbook stuff. Halfheartedly he coughed and muffled it with an open hand, but felt clumsy and so readable. It was obvious to both of them he was about to make a dictate. With a shrug of the shoulder that said, *Hell, you know what I'm up to,* to Si, he offered the dictate: "Take it easy. You've earned your time. I don't know of anything so goddamn important you've got to get all involved in it now. You must be driving Phyllis absolutely nuts. And she thought it was going to be easy!" An image of Si's wife floated to him from a distant corner of the station. He could see her pale blue eyes looking inquisitively at both of them, her head shaking in either frustration or impatience, and finally, as it always had come about, the relenting smile which had become part of her make-up, had become part of her life as the wife of *Ars Punctilio*. It had to go with the territory.

"She still doesn't like my truck, Noel. Thinks I think I'm still a kid." The big red F350, a massive ball of power that Phyllis at times thought was right at the cutting edge of senility and a thought which she invariably let go from whence it came, was parked right outside the window of the office where Silas was working his way through the Cochran case for the umpteenth time. He held up the old *Item* headline and the chief had instant memory of the case, the classic and perfect crime of the century, still unsolved after fifty years. A flicker of passionate disgust passed through him as a few of the old details came into his mind. Most of all, as a man first, and then as a cop, it was the garroting that had inflamed him long ago, which came back on him so quickly and just as strong as it had previously been. The evil was liquid on him, crawling on his skin, his mouth foul and dry. He wished he could see into Silas' head, to see how things stacked up in that fertile mind, to mark what he had marked, even so early in the game. They'd been through so much crap together, but the garroting was something by itself. He thought, as he had before, it was a maniac leaving some kind of clue to his identity, an aberrant signature of an aberrant mind. Silas nodded when the chief made that thought verbal; it registered with a big check mark because he too had had that same intuition. The cut of the cloth was evident in each.

"So," continued the chief, "what are you up to?"

Silas looked up at his old partner. The jaw of Noel Rebenkern was still square, but the neck was thicker and somewhat softer, the hair thinner on top, and the steel blue of his eyes had watered a bit. Their thoughts could have been in unison: he'd been through a number of hells with this man, starting way out in the islands of the Pacific almost half a century ago when each was a mere boy, through the silent agonies and noisy carnage that had spawned themselves off Route One and its fast world, the speed lane that halved Saugus. Silas thought, *My old pal won't be long behind me when I leave this post.*

"I'm going to give it a whirl, Noel," he said, "one last swing through the hinterlands as they might say. There's got to be something they didn't pay attention to, some little idiosyncrasy left untouched , smoldering all these years, perhaps a piece of matter so small or so insignificant it didn't appear to matter at all."

His forehead V'd itself as if pointing right down his distinguished Roman nose, the flesh of his inquisitiveness furrowed deeply. It was evident to the chief that his old comrade was poring over every detail with the same old determination his whole career had been marked with, for he was a computer in himself, a forty-five-year-old filing system, and was possessed of a filter that caught at the most minute bit of slag and slush one could imagine. *Whoever you are, my weird soul of souls, beware if you're not dead, if you didn't die out on the islands when we were there, if you didn't join up after killing that poor girl and get wasted in the hell of Europe, if you're still kicking around Lynn* all *these years later, I don't give a shit how old you are now, you better beware!*

Silas' eyes had darkened, the skin on the lower part of his face tighter than it had been minutes ago, still wearing the russet cordage of the weather and the years, almost a sandpaper quality to that organ. There was a *lock* about him, a fusion of all his parts coming into one feeling, one sense, one duty. He'd been that way ever since the chief had known him, a determination that seemed to take over every facet of his being, the bulldog cop taking a grip and never letting go until some kind of accomplishment had been made.

"Do you want some time away from here, Si?

"Don't treat me special, Noel. I didn't ask for that." They were eye to eye, superior to subordinate, friend to friend.

The chief reddened a bit. "For Christ's sake, Si, you are special! You've done your damn job better than any man could have, better than I could have. We both know that. I just got through the paper work a little easier, so don't give me any of this happy horseshit you appear to be swinging around here. Take all the time you want. Take off the blue if you want. Go plain. Go where you want. Dig in where you want. We both know the cut-off date. So does Phyllis. If you got to do this, do it." He let his stomach sag back against his belt and let out a mouthful of breath, unmistakably a period at the end of a sentence.

It was settled then, cut and pasted; Silas Tully set about to solve a nearly fifty-year-old murder. The distaste was still in his mouth as he thought about the golden anniversary coming up in 1991. Frances Cochran, nineteen, pretty dark-haired bookkeeper from Lynn, bludgeoned, burned, beat to absolute hell by a fiendish madman, garroted finally in some grotesque measure he could not fathom in all of human kind, lay dead almost fifty years, and his own marker, his forty-fifth and final year on the Saugus Police Department, was also coming to its own celebration.

Time and duty of the most inordinate order came at him and took hold of him. Into overdrive he went, calling on adrenaline when he needed it, rarely resting, and testing Phyllis to the limit. Through every resource available, he went back through the case. Police files, through a compassionate network of the brotherhood, found their way to him from Lynn and Swampscott and Salem, and from departments as far west as Idaho where one suspect had been apprehended, and Ohio where another man was once questioned, and also there came files from the district attorney's office, and musty documentation from the coroners' offices, for poor Frances had been exhumed and a second autopsy performed on August 8 of that eventful year of 1941. All the suspects, and there were a lot who had been questioned, were re-studied. He pored over those who had been recently released from prisons and were known to have been around the area at the time of Frances' death. And there were musicians and cooks and students and street people and acquaintances and neighbors and cabbies that had been queried. There was the car, a square backed car spotted by at least two witnesses who had seen Frances get into it on a side street off Eastern Avenue, square-backed Chevy, '31-'35, with yellow wooden spokes on its wheels, perhaps with yellow trimming, and driven by a male whom she had obviously known.

In the first twenty-five years after the murder there had been more than twenty confessions, all fizzling out, falling off into the dream world that some people have to inhabit, or have to cook up for themselves. Rewards had been offered over the years, lots of them, from a variety of sources and for a variety of reasons. Silas was quite sure some of them had been offered because there really appeared to be no chance to solve the case. That disturbed him also. He could not stomach anybody making points on somebody else's pain, let alone most atrocious murder. When the image of the garrote came on him again, he determined to find out what kind of a man would do that kind of act. Whenever he went away from the act, something brought him back to it. He paid attention to that fact, much as he did everything else. Nothing was going to escape him. Nothing at all!

An inch wide the stick had been. And lethal in its own right! It made him shiver. He remembered Joe Dixon and Joe Ditson long ago after the war and after they had come out of a Japanese POW camp. Their stories had made him shiver, too. Every now and then he'd catch himself in a weird and frightful reverie of their plight and of Frances' plight. His skin would crawl with the known terrors. His resolve grew in proportion.

Phyllis began to relent. Her smile came up more readily.

December eventually came howling down out of the Maritimes, the snow drifting at times nearly five feet high across schoolyards and playgrounds and at other times shutting Route One down to a minor crawl. Silas Tully was like a ship on the lone sea of a month of storms, moving anywhere and everywhere in that redoubtable red truck of his, high slung, ground-clearing, ominous in its power, red as a fire bomb, taking winter head on, as it had not been taken on before by a proximal retiree. On his way at times he remembered the awesome and orange Walter Snowfighters of the Eastern Mass. Bus Company and how they had kept much of the North Shore roads clear of snow back there in the days when Frances could have seen them. He passed by places where clear-cut and exact pictures came back to him, full of details and all the background in place, places he had known, obviously places that Frances had known too. He felt driven. His recall was working in top order and damned if he wouldn't show retirement itself a thing or two, if he had to die trying.

Before long every cop in Lynn and Salem intimately knew of him and his mission, and when he passed by their beats or their stations or dropped in again to get the name of a still-living retired cop who might have heard a word or two, they smiled and muttered small asides about senility and Alzheimer's disease, but still held out one last long and thin line of hope for him. They shared the blue charge, and though he may have been against the windmills, they quietly acknowledged his mission and his drive.

One of them was a bright young cop from Lynn who had graduated from Salem State. His name was Rick Sanborn and he had read about the case and let much of it filter through his mind. Nothing showed itself to him, nothing that held any light, but after much thought, he came to a conclusion and called Silas Tully about it. What he offered was nothing more than what Noel Rebenkern had offered, the fact of the garroting.

"I know it might sound odd to you, Mr. Tully, but that thing with the stick really bothers me. I think it's the most interesting thing there is to discuss. Nothing I can add, or discuss any more than this, but I swear it talks to me when I think about it. Something so apparent about it we can't see it. I feel it in my bones. It's dark and unnatural, as if the devil himself was in on it. You might think I'm crazy or something, but it really hangs on me. I know I've only been around a short time and you're an old hand at all of this, but I just had to tell you how it bugs me all the time. Even when I was in school at Salem State, and I'd be thinking of old cases or tough cases you kind of hear about, this one kept coming at me."

They had had a number of discussions about the case. The youngster was adamant, though quite unsure why he was so homed in on the awful stick. Silas Tully kept a track record of the garrote image. The way it continually reared its ugly head did not go unnoticed.

When the preponderance of his gathered facts began to tip itself sideways, threatened to spill itself all over itself, he plotted and laid out a graph. Everything he knew he put onto that graph, and after a hundred attempts of making verticals and horizontals show some attachment or connection, revising the very structure with each attempt, every revision becoming a little clearer, he began to see all the tangibles and intangibles in a different light. No one, he knew, had ever seen what he had seen; at least, not from this perspective. That it was merely a different view, a different focus, was not lost on him at first, because somewhere under his eyes, somewhere on the spread of the page, a single clue might leap out of darkness, one lone bulb or candle glow in the utter darkness of the mystery, one fallible and untested little item would come forward that would unscrew a murder now fifty years unsolved and still counting.

In January of that extra tough winter both Phyllis and the chief were on him to slow down, not to quit outright, but to slow down. "Fat chance I'll have at Florida!" Phyllis said when he came late for supper for the third day in a row. "It'll close on empty before we know it. You'll fall over at that damn desk of yours or behind the wheel of that truck and it'll be all over." But even as she said it, she tempered it and laid a soft hand across his shoulder, tapping home her love. One thing Silas Tully always noticed were the small signals left out in the air or in the corner of a room for the taking, a sigh, a tap, a look another soul might never catch a glimpse of, the huge and ponderous world and all of life beating its way at the smallest edge. He heard the microwave's new-tech signal, electronic, radar-related, almost mystic in its new-age music, sounding as if something had been decoded, broken down, and realized she'd been watching for him all the while, as she always did. The warmth of the house slid around him like a favorite jacket taken down from an old nail in the back hallway.

Noel Rebenkern, always from some distance watching his old comrade and compatriot, at least understood the drive and the compulsion targeting Silas Tully. He'd spoken once to Reed Clanberry, as Reed rolled himself out from under a cruiser whose transmission had pissed the bed, hydraulic fluid a red stain over a good portion of his shirt and his hands as black as baked potatoes in a camp fire. "What the hell I'm afraid of is that he won't get to his friggin' retirement at all. He'll just close shop one day and check his badge. It'll be all done, and Phyllis will come down here and we'll have a nice chat and she'll go away from here red-eyed and he'll be gone off with all the others." Talking to Reed always helped him, for Reed was always on his back or on his butt while working on one of the cruisers in the police garage, down and dirty in his support of brother officers, though his bent was machines, how they ran, what the theories said they should do.

"He's a big boy, chief," said the elongated and prone Reed, still laid back on the roller, the near seven feet of him hanging over the small roller like one of the Three Stooges on a child's bed. "So let him have his way at this latest escapade. He ain't been wrong but once I know of, and we didn't want to celebrate that one too much. Just let old Jarhead go his way. If it's there, if anything's there, he'll bring it home."

Noel Rebenkern nodded and walked off. It was cut and pasted. Even the damn mechanic had the good-to-the-bone feeling about

Silas. He walked off, pulling at his belt line for the second serious time in one day. The skinny, overly long mechanic had unsettled him. *Damn, I ought to know better that that!* In the corridor between the garage and his office his words had no hollowness to them. From then on he would keep his mouth shut. What the hell! His own retirement was not that far off either. Either one of them, Silas or him, could slide into oblivion on the greased skids, as long as nothing came out of the woodwork to scald the town manager or the board of selectmen, as long as nothing could screw up the works. Saugus was, normally, a quiet town split by the pike, having its own brand of politics, its own nirvana this side of Boston and that side of Manchester-by-the-Sea and Prides Crossing and the dollar signs sitting behind stone walled estates.

The reveries were coming on him again. They were rather serious now, full-blown pictures of those other times, and the feelings that went with them. Such moments might have frightened him if the anchor of Silas was not always a part of those reveries; good old Silas, jawed-down Silas, bulldog Silas, comrade. The old sentiments piled on top of one another and he realized Silas had made life most interesting, had colored it for him, and had drawn from him the highest comparisons every step of the way. Even as he walked away from the long mechanic, those thoughts came on him again; he pictured Silas, for the umpteenth thousandth time, poring over details, his mind locked down to one microbial trail, pulling straight with him an array of genes and DNAs, and the chief thought of being in the fourth row of Dodger Stadium the year before, and Pavarotti, alone even with the other two tenors, looking on, getting ready to sing *Nessum Dorma.* In a quick moment of change he then compared his old friend to Denver's John Elway stepping up to the line, down six points, thirty-eight seconds to go, the ball on his own 38 yard line. *Piece of cake!*

Clarity and reality hit him as he thought of Frances Cochran and her crushed head and battered face and immolated body. An utter helplessness came over him. He thought all there was left for her was Silas Tully, like Pavarotti getting ready, Elway about to make something happen. A jolt of unnerving energy flushed through his body, carrying him away from comparisons. *All there was left for her was Silas Tully!*

Silas Tully, for all the thoughts and considerations and condemnations of his task, for all the small asides strewn in his path or beside it, for all the occasional almost-suppressed laughter that trickled in his passing wake like weak-kneed commentaries, kept at it. Again and again and again, for long days on end and weeks on end, he kept at it. And the terribly long winter passed and spring seeped onto the land. Freshness and a new eagerness not thought possible came on him just as the land swelled with newness of its own. On him had also come a few clarifications expressing themselves with all their own vigor: (1) whoever that foul murderer was, he must have at one time been in the wide and circuitous net which the police had cast out after the discovery of poor Frances' body, a net which swung as wide as Idaho and Ohio, a net which had caught up fellow students and neighbors and itinerants and those usual suspects who had records or who had been recently released from prison and he had been let out of that net because of a perfected alibi or other reason; and (2) the act of the garroting itself which he could not shake. No matter how hard he tried, he could not dissuade himself that there was nothing insignificant about the employment of the horrible stick. If the stick had been used before she had been bludgeoned, he surmised, she would have been dead anyway, or close to it, and there would have been no reason for smashing her head open. If her head had been smashed first, there would have been no reason to garrote her. He made it that simple to himself. That the killer was maniacal did not say he was stupid, for he had eluded the police for half a century, *if he was not dead, if he had not died out there on a Pacific beach, if he had not died in Marine garb in a Marine firefight. No way! Never a Marine!*

Late April had come and the new smells were everywhere, and the chief's boat, *Just Too Blue,* was in the water of the

Saugus River, right near the penciled memorial stone erected
for another police officer downed in his tracks. Silas had spent
a lot of time over the years fishing on the craft with Noel or
just beering-out out there on the Atlantic, away from phones
and the traffic and the mayhem, aging themselves on the ageless
sea. Now retirement was rearing its head for good and the
dreadful punches of time came at him, coming brutal and bony
and downhill all the way, punching their way into his abrupt
consciousness at times, walking him to the edge. Retirement
might be like a death sign.

Frances, gasping for air, choking, pain riding her body like a
malevolent lover, was with him every second of his wakeful hours
and had obviously been with him as he slept. Her grip was frightful
and grew more ominous. Phyllis felt it, he felt it. Unknown sources
in his body made demands on him, sometimes twisted him and he
fought to maintain his equilibrium, his sense of purpose, his life-
long effort of trying to be personally uninvolved with crime and
its victims. In this case it did not work. There was something else,
he did not feel blameless and that bothered him.

Wanting a new perspective, a new lift to go along with new
raw feelings, he borrowed *Just Too Blue* for a day and sat, anchor
down, out near Egg Rock, the mound of granite rising from the
bay off King's Beach where he could look back at Lynn. The tide
rolled under him. Time rolled under him. The agony was no less
and no clearer out on the cool surface. He wished he could look
back omnisciently at one piece of a clue, a small piece of any clue,
the single strand of red hair found on her body, the car with the
yellow wheel spokes, a tire track left undetected, a footprint, a
thumb print. If only he could look into the minds of the suspects,
still believing that he had once been in the net.

And the garrote came back to him there on the wide sea.

Visibly, willfully, he turned from it, shunting it aside. His graph
was spread out on the deck, the awfully intricate grid of lines
seeming to go unconnected and crazily in every direction. But
somehow the lines came plotted to him and a number of variables

of their connections appeared readable. He wanted to tighten some screws, but futility came at him. On the high sea, the endless water spreading behind him as if going on to infinity, chances were slim to none at catching that blackguard murderer. They were like the chances of finding one wave in the unending series of waves rolling under him to be a special wave. Here Silas knew himself to be a very minor drop of matter in this vastness, as well as in the matter of this business of solution. For a moment he felt overwhelmed by his own tininess, one small wave among the thousands and thousands of waves, until the thought came to him that for Frances Cochran, fifty years dead, forgotten by so many, so many of her peers gone, her parents long gone, he was the only hope, the last hope of resolve.

From there on the face of the Atlantic, the continuity of life itself rising and falling underneath him, underneath the keel, he looked back over Lynn and the death of the girl and all the information which he had come across and which now lay in turmoil in his mind, though sketched and gridded on his pad of paper. He saw himself back at the station going over the matter, and at home probably driving poor Phyllis nuts, and plying his way through snow and rain and hail to get more information and wearing his welcome thin no matter where he went. He saw his tracks crossing and crisscrossing all the North Shore and points beyond. He saw the exodus of thousands of young men for the war of wars, and, unknown to him at the moment, with that exodus he would come to see one strange-eyed young man in the act of escape.

He saw the enormity of the sea and the task.

And he came back to the garrote again! Or it came to him! It would not go away.

The grid lines of his graph fell under his eyes. All the names of all the suspects fell under his eyes. Poring over each one, each one became a personality, and he sought a chink in the armor. Then, on that wide and limitless sea, on that great expanse, like he was a thimble afloat on eternity, he had a new idea. It burst upon him!

The engine cranked into life and the sound immediately seemed to be swallowed up by the enormity about him. But he headed for the Saugus River and Noel's slip at the yacht club.

Mere hours later he was poring over old issues of the *Lynn Item* looking for photos. A few came to light of the type he was searching for. Here and there, at that time with war starting shortly after Frances' death, lots of young men enlisted and photos were shown of neighborhood friends and teammates and other groups going off to war together. In one small photo of a dozen men, all of them exuberant and smiling in ignorance at the adventure waiting on them, one face was downcast, averting that intimate exchange of gazes that's called for by the photographer. The young man could not have made himself any smaller, any darker, any more secretive, and any more obvious! His name was not given, but that would pose no great problem, thought Silas. Most of them were French Basque. The Raiders from Boston Street where it abruptly found Flax Pond.

Whatever took him to the Boston Public Library to search for information on Basque witchcraft, until this day he cannot fully explain, except that the boy with the averted look, and the very act of garroting itself, had somehow been grounded in the reach of the Basque as it touched on him.

In his studied research he read about the *bruxos* and the *xorguinos,* Basque men and women who practiced witchcraft and black magic in the Province of Gupuzcoa along the Bay of Biscay, and in the mountain range of Amboto where they still talk about the Lady of the Caves, and her ointments of pulverized toads and a Basque herb called *usainbelar.* All about the witches he read, immersed for hours and hours in the spread of Iberia, the bays, the mountains, and he almost leapt up from his seat at a description of a Basque witch being killed. It was a vivid description of how she was first strangled with a stick thrust down her throat and then she was burned at the stake or thrust into a barrel of tar or pitch and if she got loose from the stake or got out the barrel, she was thrust back into the fire. And he found an old passage, so shockingly similar, about witches' executions in the highlands of Scotland, which made him leap once again in his seat. "… *and thay was sticket in the throte with a garruote and thay wer brunt quick eftir sic ane crewell maner, than sum of thame deit in desspair, renunce and blaspheme and; and utheris half brunt brake out of the fyre and wes cast quick in it agane, quhill thay wer brunt* all *thay daith.* "

Silas could picture all of it, and its horror charged over him. So many innocents had been executed this way in countless villages and towns of the Old World. And it had come to America, it had come to Salem right down the street, and, he was further convinced, it had come just down the road in Lynn to poor Frances Cochran.

The Red Raider with the averted eyes was not difficult to identify, nor was his military history, and three weeks later, after Silas' request for information about the young man's basic outfit was printed in the *Legionnaire's Magazine*, he had a damn good picture of what Lamon L'Supprenant was all about. And he was still living. In Salem. A Basque. Into, well into, the occult, into sorcery, into black magic, and the *bruxos,* and the *xorguinos.* He wondered about the *garrote.* But, furthermore, L'Supprenant had been a redhead in his early days, and one of three redheads who were questioned.

His uncle, he also found out, had been a cop.

In the service, in a Division Headquarters Company of the U.S. 7th Infantry Division, a vital force in the Pacific war, a long time in the islands, brought out of there to Korea later on, L'Supprenant'd been a strange chicken, full of wild and woolly things, and he was remembered for his strangeness by some old comrades. Of the three who wrote back to Silas, not one questioned why information was being sought, and Silas interpreted that to mean each one of them might have thought, even after all these years, that Lamon L'Supprenant needed explaining. Only one person could be approached with all this information, flimsy and outrageous as it was, and that was Noel Rebenkern, chief, comrade, and friend, though the last qualifier could certainly be strained by something as touchy as this case and the parameters it was at, fifty years of grayness and obliqueness. But chinks appearing!

He told Noel all he knew, all of the Basque's history, as it had come revealed to him, and brought it right down to the single strand of red hair, and the picture of the Red Raiders going off to war.

Noel might have leaped on him. "You got to be crazy, Si! You can't go anyplace with all that crap. Jesus, man, if Danvers State Hospital was still open you'd be there on the hill before you could blow your nose. They'd put you in a white jacket and take you down a long corridor. And they'd throw the friggin' key away!" He kept shaking his head as if disbelief was all around him, and his eyes went opaque and then a queasy gray. More of his age showed, more than he wanted to show.

Gathering himself, he added, "There's no legitimate way to present any of it. All the work you've done could go right down the tube. No!" he added vociferously, slamming his fist on the desk, "you haven't got a chance in hell!" He looked at Silas' face. It was not unnerved, not upset, not in any sort of quandary. His lifetime fiend, Silas Tully, was a kid again. "What the hell are you going to do with all of this?"

The soon-to-be-gone policeman looked him in the eye. "I'm going to smoke him out!" Something beyond affirmation was in his voice, beyond definition. By God, he had become younger! A sparkle was in his eyes. His skin had a tingle and a shine to it. His mouth was as firm as he could ever remember it.

"Si, he's got to be about seventy years old now. He'll probably have a heart attack if you go right at him. If he's the right guy, that is. That's like fish in the barrel."

"You mean you don't think we should go after him, that we shouldn't have gone after the German war criminals no matter how old they were, time served being enough for killing six million Jews. You got to be kidding me, Noel!"

"What I mean, Si, is you can't go lambasting after him with no hard proof. You'd get killed in court. He's got rights and the

burden's on us." He said *us* the only way he could, being a party
to the whole thing. "One thing else I'll say. There are a lot of guys
our age who've been obsessed with this murder, who've been
obsessed since the day it happened. It grates on them as much as
anything else, and I'll tell you why I think that's so."

Pausing, knowing the value of the caesura, trying to provide
room for everything to sink into his determined, and obviously
obsessed, comrade, he continued, his hair a bit grayer, his neck
a bit thicker, his belt line, too: "You've got to look at the time
period, Si. It was just before Pearl Harbor, and things were calm
somewhat, even though Europe was in turmoil. It was a special
time, especially for women, with things on the upswing all around;
Prohibition gone, the New Deal at work, things getting better
for the house. It was a special time indeed. Why, I've known a
bunch of guys, a lot of them from the Brickyard in Lynn, who
said their doors were never locked at night before the war. You
just didn't worry. All the big brothers were around and girls
didn't worry so much. When the war started, they tell me,
especially the guys from the Brickyard, with all the big brothers
off to war and a bunch of creeps around, they began to lock
their doors. They had to. Times began to change. Right after
Pearl Harbor, times began to change. All those guys from around
here thought about Frances Cochran for a long time, out on the
islands, in Europe, under the frigging waters of both oceans,
like somebody had cut into their space and violated one of their
own. It really pissed them off, like their kid sister had been
grabbed. A lot of them told me, with all the advanced training
they got, bayonet drills and all that stuff, they'd've killed the
son of a bitch in a second if they'd've caught him. Even old
Teddie BB in Cliftondale told me once he couldn't remember
how many times he thought about Frances when he was alone
on guard duty way the hell up there in the goddamn Aleutians.
He used to talk about it with Dashiel Hammet who was in his
outfit, on Sitka I think. Said they used to come up with some
great stories about it and how the son of a bitch could be caught

and strung up by his you-know-whats. You know what, every now and then when we take a ride after church on Sunday or on the way to a ball game down that way, he'll drive by the place. He still gets pissed, I tell you!"

Eventually, near talked out, both sides presented, they could have drawn a line in the sand, if there had been any sand in the chief's office. Peace was made and Si was going to do it his way. He had bit it off and chewed it up.

Smoking him out, to Silas Tully, was not a strange and roundabout approach. First, for a few months, he got to know Lamon L'Supprenant from behind the windshield of the big red truck and now and then the little car he had got for Phyllis. Everywhere L'Supprenant went, Silas was right behind him; and sometimes, knowing the routine so well, he was in front of him. A smoky and dark side of L'Supprenant became obvious. Not much of what he did was done openly, much of it behind locked doors in the company of likewise dark and furtive friends. That they practiced some kind of witchcraft or sorcery or black magic was evident, and that they took great profits in it showed as well, too. To Silas' trained eye the access to any of the half dozen places where things happened, were strictly controlled and under guard. He could only hazard guesses as to what might take place behind such cover.

But guesswork did not have to wait long. On July 18, 1991, fifty years almost to the day that Frances Cochran was killed, the body of a girl was found in the tall grass alongside the Happy Valley Golf Course in Lynn. Her head had been crushed, her jaw smashed, her clothing torn from her mutilated body. Also, a small wooden stick similar to a tent peg had been stuck down her throat. She too had been garroted! And a single strand of red hair was found on her body. Laboratory DNA tests showed that it matched the strand of red hair found on Frances Cochran's body fifty years earlier.

The city of Lynn went berserk. Police said there was not a single clue besides the strand of red hair; no witnesses to the deed, no sounds in the night, no suspicious activities along Lynnfield

Street, and, this time, no car with yellow wheels. The connections were obvious and a sweeping terror started throughout the city.

Noel Rebenkern, in his office, faced Silas. "If you get him on this one, you've got him on the first. There'll be no question. I just wished we'd've done something sooner. Now, don't you feel bad. I'm the one who put the reins on you."

"I'm willing to bet that that poor kid knew this son of a bitch from some place. Maybe from one of those damn places I couldn't get into. Or if she didn't know him, she knew one of his young friends."

"You mean like an acolyte or an apprentice getting some OJT! Jayzuz, what the hell have they got going?"

His head shook back and forth in disbelief. He felt a lot older than he had earlier in the day. "Well, Si, I guess it has to be your shot. How you want to call it. You know those guys from Lynn will be calling you, not a bit of doubt about that. They won't have those silly little grins on their kissers now." His face lit up a bit as he added, "Unless they think you've got something to do with it." His guffaw filled the room.

"Thanks for the memories," answered Si. Then he nodded, and looked a poser for a short time, then looked at the chief and said, "Some more smoking out, but this time with contact. " And he explained what he was going to do to loosen Lamon L'Supprenant from his hold on life.

For four days in a row after the discovery of Angel Corkery's body at the Happy Valley Golf Course, and after the Lynn chief asked him to come down to see him sometime, the following typewritten notes, each one on successive days, were mailed by Silas Tully to Lamon L'Supprenant at his Salem address:

1. I used to think Frances was the only one.

2. When you find out who I am, I'll be waiting for you, but not at all as innocent as Frances or Angel. I'll be a lot stronger and a lot meaner.

3. You ever try that stick on me, that sick garrote, I'll put it to you where the sun don't shine.

4. I don't care how old you are, you are going to pay! Nothing is going to help you now, not the Lady of the Caves or your crushed toad skins or your usainbelar or any of your acolytes or apprentices. You, my evil one, are due, and Frances and Angel, God rest their sweet souls, may have some peace once again.

When Lamon L'Supprenant tried to bolt, in the middle of the night, a young man with him, and bags of mysterious goods piled onto the back seat and into the trunk, Silas Tully and Lynn police officer Rick Sanborn and two Salem cops were there to grab them. In one of the parcels confiscated from the L'Supprenant car, police found a decorative box with two *X's cut* into the cover and eight more strands of red hair gathered inside, all the same source, all from Lamon L'Supprenant. They also found a ritual of avenge which detailed the garroting and murder of a L'Supprenant relative which had happened a hundred and fifty years earlier in France. Lila of the Caves had gotten the promise of revenge from her sons, from her descendants.

It was only a Saugus cop who had stood in the way of another four hundred years of sacrifices, one every fifty years.

Almost Rickshaw

M aye Tuong was part Chinese, had three brothers and one sister, all married and moved out, and lived with her mother and father across the Saugus River, at the upper end where a small wooden bridge spanned the water. Her mother was the Chinese parent, not the father, Henry Tuong, who was, as far as I knew, an old Lynn boy from way back who brought his wife home from one of his wars as a Marine. Shanghai rang a bell but I was never sure of where. I did know some other things about Maye, fact or fiction as you'll have it, which had settled into my mind because she was extremely shapely for one thing, and she never had a date, at least I never saw her with a fellow. One time in the past, I heard, she'd been embarrassed at the beach when someone spotted a patch of thick, black hair on her backside, just below her waistline. A small patch it was, but a patch out of place. A few tough and pointed wisecracks were tossed off at that time and Maye was never seen at the beach again, never seen in a bathing suit again. I was one of those who never saw Maye at the beach or in a bathing suit. I never saw that thick, black, out-of-place patch either, but had thought about it, I'm willing to bet, on a daily occurrence, perhaps hourly if you're aware of the routine. Maye, on this night when the story really began, was 28 years old, or thereabouts, having unsettled some of my recent and late night thoughts, the older woman kind that haunt and capture and beset the young mind: *let me teach you a thing or two, young man, you naughty boy, you.*

Oh, I could glory in the opportunities coming my way.

Now, on this night, not far from the historical Iron Master's House of the First Iron Works of America, I heard people talking in the darkness beside a parked car, a girl's voice and a man's voice, more than whispers, but exclusive all the while. When the talk ended the car drove off, the engine still purring. The girl began to walk away. From the first sound of her heels on the street pavement, I knew who she was. A short thirty feet later she turned off the street and walked down the path toward the river, toward her parents' house with one window upstairs. Her heels clicked again on the narrow wooden bridge spanning the Saugus River only thirty feet wide at that point, the old Scott's Mill and the dam locks sitting close by.

Maye Tuong was twice as old as me. I was a fourteen-year old freshman in high school and she had been catching my eye for almost a year. I didn't really know why that was happening, though the exploration was enjoyable, at times exciting, blood flow at early expression. When she walked, which was just about every place she went in town, her hips made me think about boats hitched to a slack rope at the tide change, where the river and the ocean met three miles downstream. I did not yet have a name for that rhythm but it carried a music making impressions without sound. In close association a near-hum sat by my ear, calling for measurement, for some act of completion or satisfaction. In a pale green dress she wore at least once a week, if not twice, her backside shivered subtly and shook itself with each step. An awakening excitement accompanied those seemingly menial tremors. And I was ready to swear, in secret of course, that Maye was the one woman I knew of who could ride the night wind like a butterfly with scent. Private belief told me I was the only one beholden to these observations, as if they existed only for me and, justly, because of me.

Quickly I rehashed all I'd just seen and heard, and made

judgments, bringing in to play all that I knew. The big sedan, the first time I observed it in my end of town, had been idling in the thick darkness beneath a tunnel of elm trees all at spring bloom and hurrying for summer. The engine purr came to me when I was about a hundred feet away, the sound subtle, almost secretive, providing no identity at all. I could not tell the make of it, not Chevy tappets, not a Ford whine, not a Pontiac universal or noisy drive shaft. At the side of the road it was parked, partly on the unpaved sidewalk, where a post and rail fence sat for more than three hundred feet along a steep embankment falling away to the river, and the overgrown site of the First Iron Works of America— marsh grass, saw grass, reeds taller than fences, a few acres of cat'o'nines, all hiding the old histories. Lately, though, for the first time ever, strangers had been crawling around the place, all over the slag pile where for years we had played and mined the glassy black chunks of slag, and in and out of the Ironmaster's House still standing, the one Henry Ford almost bought and shipped to Dearborn, Michigan, and stepping off plotting paces on the slope toward the river. There had been talk of the whole site being recovered from time, possibly being reconstructed. Some of the men, we heard, were from Harvard College, others from big business. There was talk of a lot of money on hand, most of it coming from major steel companies with deep-seated interests in the iron industry.

As a fourteen-year-old I always walked home in the dark from Saugus Center, perhaps no more than a half mile, but a walk whose history crowded me with images. That walk took me past the town hall and the library, a couple of churches, an odd lot of houses, past the site of America's first successful iron works, circa 1636, and through dark passages under old elms the blight had not yet touched. One of the houses was the old McCullough house still sporting inside Indian shutters at the kitchen windows, and the old boathouse dancehall out behind that had collapsed one night, sending the piano sliding across the floor where it lay rotting still. Another structure was the rebuilt parson's house where the parson's depraved son burned alive one night a half century earlier. The darkness along a goodly stretch of that road was conclusive, shutting out any and all lights from the Center, from the other few houses along the way, from the edge of civilization, and shutting out even a piece of a moon coming over the top of Vinegar Hill. Now and then, near the end of my walk along the river's edge, always toward midnight, I'd see, or hear ahead of me or behind me, her heels clicking, Maye Tuong coming home from work at the telephone company. Maye always walked, being athletic and too poor to have a car, and always alone, never having a boyfriend that I had ever seen or heard about.

She carried mystery on the air.

This night the big car had stopped, two people talked lightly, Maye and whoever, and then they went on their ways. A week later I saw the same thing, only this time I knew who the car belonged to, the big Cadillac with a hood long as the canal at Salter's Mill and generally as quiet as the stars sitting over my shoulder on many nights. The owner of the vehicle was Harvey Upham, a heavyweight in town. He owned two stores, served on one town governing board or another for twenty or more years, had a pretty talented and athletic son, and a wife who was crippled and bed-ridden. She had been that way for at least a dozen years. Harvey was in his mid-forties, pretty good looking, and had tons of energy. And nobody ever said anything bad about him, what with the way he took care of his wife, went to all the practices and games his son played in, was an all-'round damn nice guy who did a bunch of all-'round damn nice things for the town. If people wondered about his night life, I never heard a word, though now I had a few odd thoughts playing around in my mind, created by these casual conversations, under the elms, against the fence, in the dark.

Of course, those were the days when I began my own expeditions and explorations, probably starting the day that Ginnie Dumont straddled a log in the woods when we were coming back from a dip in the pond and I saw her white underpants as clear as

I'd ever imagined. A short time later, when she managed to squirm around, with minor abandon I figured, I saw what they had been hiding, her own little garden of growth and dark as clouds. I am afraid I was off and running that day, and Maye Tuong and Harvey Upham slid away from my consciousness, though every few days I did see his car moving around town and managed to see her memorable walk on a few occasions as she went about her business. The moves of her aft end could stop traffic, you could almost see her flesh rippling under cover, and her scent was unmistakable. Oh, Maye, oh may I, Maye?

One day, in late August, when I was on the football team and we were practicing at the stadium, Harvey Upham sat in the bleachers, as always, with a couple of other pals who were town businessmen, watching pre-season practice from the stands. Harvey's son Rex was a pretty good running back and used to light up every scrimmage. I would see Harvey stand and shake his fist in the air over a good run. His pals, the two Ryeman brothers who ran a car agency, did the same thing, all hooting and hollering as though they were at a real game. They were the only men I knew who did not have to report to work every day at a job, having the wherewithal to be wherever they wanted.

On one of those early scrimmage days, way off in the corner of the field, practically out of sight of everybody else, I caught a quick glimpse of Maye Tuong. She had been standing beside a tree at the far corner of the field, the most distant point, and her dress was perfect camouflage. She had stepped away from the tree and bent over to pick up something. I recognized her pale green dress, the one she often wore. In one near dream she had slipped out of it in a slice of guile I had never seen, but not once showing me her backside and the legendary curse. At practice this day she did look nice in pale green, surrounded by leaves, at the edge of the pond, at the far end of the field, practically on the next planet. Of course, she couldn't have seen much from that distance, but to me it came more as a statement of support, or curiosity.

One or the other I'd guessed. *Hey, Harvey, I know what else holds your interest.*

That scene sparked my imagination again, about Harvey and Maye saying hello in the dark. It was always in the same dark stretch of road, with only one house at one end of that patch of night and nothing but railing on the other side, and then the steep drop down to reeds and wetlands of the river's edge where peepers, in romantic weather, held choir practice, along with frogs of all sizes and ranges. Even though I saw the same scene a couple of more times, their simple hello in the dark, nothing much else happened. But I was thinking about such things all the time, having lately told a girl named Ethel she was *the most beautiful thing I had ever seen in my whole entire life.*

All this time, of course, there was talk about Mrs. Upham's condition. At the news store you'd hear how poorly she was doing, how some friends began to measure time for her, and a few casual comments about how Harvey had to be so damn strong because any other man would be driven to madness. I let a little of that sink into me, but not all of it. There was Ginnie Dumont's pants getting whiter and fainter and finally disappearing one day, before or after Ethel I am not sure, and the thought that Maye Tuong's dark and thick patch of black hair, misplaced as it was, had a classic sense of mystery about it. There were nights I could swear it was visible to me if I closed my eyes. I'd see it move. See it stretch. See it wink at me, the way such things wink, day and night, morn and eve, every few seconds it seemed. And in a grasp at eternal attention it had an aroma that could incite the most horrific senses ever to be exaggerated.

Maye, all that time, came up from the river house on her way to work at the telephone office more than a mile away. In bad weather, once in a while, she'd get a ride from one of the neighbors. For one stretch of four winter months, another operator sat waiting at the top of the river road to give Maye a ride to work. Then, in the first days of spring, Maye was walking again. Perhaps her driver had moved or been married, but I never saw her again. In that time Ethel moved on and so did Ginnie Dumont, the way people pass in and out of our lives. The one constant was Maye Tuong and her mysterious patch of black hair, slightly displaced; she came and went in dreams, came and went at day's beginning and at day's end, and her trek downhill to the river's edge, and the little house where she lived with her parents, a girl of poor fortune and great promise. Great promise. I couldn't stop dreaming about her.

One night, coming back from the Center, crickets and peepers filling me with high romance, the air sweeping me with new bud aromas and other scents, grass and leaves alive and all green, Harvey and Maye were talking. Their voices were soft and hushed at first and I was padding soft as an Indian. When I stopped in my tracks, I heard Harvey say, "If I could Maye, I'd pull you around town in a rickshaw, like in China, like in Shanghai or Taiwan, or any of those other places I've heard about. I'd take you to dinner at the Golden Buddha or Kowloon Island, but I can't. I'd run up and down the streets of the town pulling you behind me. I'd shout out your name. I'd shout out, 'Here's Maye Tuong, a great lady.' I'd love to do that, to show you off. You've saved my life. You deserve it, but I can't. There's.... "

A brick suddenly hit me; I didn't want to hear any more. It all came down on me. The unequivocal and demanding ministrations for his wife. It was the way my elderly uncle had made silent demands on one whole section of the family for close to nine months of painful dying and undeniable loss of an element important to him that he could not talk about. I had seen something in his eyes that he wouldn't or couldn't let go of, or it wouldn't let go of him. It was a whack right on the side of the head, one of my grandfather's infamous *one deserving goldang upside of the head*, and on my heart in the same jolt. I started back toward the Center, hearing only the peepers kissing the night and the crickets holding up their end of all things lovely. The night enveloped Maye and Harvey, and me. It was close to midnight when I got home, and the road loomed empty the whole way.

And so it was all that summer and fall, at least two nights a week, Harvey would pick Maye up in total darkness and drop her off a few hours later at the same spot, so she could walk down the path to home. She'd cross the small footbridge, her heels clicking on the wooden span, move silently along the other side through a small grass field where once the moon on top of Vinegar Hill lit her up. She'd get home to the little cape. Soon, the light would go on in the upstairs window facing the river, she'd shower, towel off, go to bed, the light a final sign as it went out. Once I thought I saw the patch of darkness at her backside. I thought it was the sexiest thing I had ever seen; it had me mesmerized.

One night, peepers and croakers working me over, my head full of visions, with a small breeze like a new lover, potable and delicious and full of caresses, I swiped a pal's dory, and rowed easily down river. In the small bend of the river nearest to Maye's house, reeds and cat'o'nines standing behind me all at attention, I slipped the anchor over the side in silence, and was closer than ever to the dream, to Maye Tuong, to the dark patch. It had never lost its grip on me.

But I had minded my own business once and walked away, and now it had gotten hold of me again. I was captivated. By degrees it worked on me, filling every night with new visions, creating others, making demands. It was frontal assault from the backside.

One night, just before midnight, Maye off with Harvey to wherever, I hung around the bridge. A faint fall coolness touched the air, a pleasantness on the skin. It carried contemplation. Above, on the road, the car stopped, merged totally with darkness. I heard the door close, heard Maye's heels for a few steps, and then knew she was on the gravel path down to the river. I coughed to let her know I was at the bridge.

She wasn't so dumb, I guess. "What are you doing, here, Tom? Still watching me? I know you've never said anything and I appreciate that. You can guess where we go and what we do. He needs me every once in a while, and for god's sake, I need him too. I never told him how you've been around. I could see you some nights. I bet my eyes are as good as yours."

I didn't want to lie. I didn't want to play games. "I keep dreaming about you," I said.

"The older woman thing, I'll bet. Well, it's your turn tonight. This will be your one and only night, and never again. Never sneak around again, not around me. He would die if he thought anyone knew. Now come over here, if you will, out of the way."

She had me by the hand and ushered me off the bridge and into a copse of trees at the river's edge. She kissed me. Her tongue was in my mouth. Immediately I was on fire. My tongue was in her mouth, my fiery tongue, tasting, being tasted back. My hands moved, and she made them move more.

"Do you think I'm beautiful?"

"Yes, I do. I keep dreaming about you."

She pulled my head down to her breast. She slid my mouth down over one nipple. "Do all the things he does for himself, but do these things for me. Make me beautiful all over, all beautiful, all over. Do it because you want to and not because you need to. Make me lovely, Tommy. Make me lovely all over."

"I want to see all of you," I said.

She almost knocked me over when she replied, "You want to see my back, don't you? He said that too, but it took him a long time to say it."

Maye spun around and was out of her dress in seconds, standing, almost modeling, in her bra and underpants. I was wishing for the moon so I could see her, and then I was glad it was not shining down on us. I was in the dark, with an older woman, a twice-as older woman. There was no fire, but I felt the fire, all the tongues of it. There was no moon; there should have been, but I didn't even hear the peepers or the crickets or any of that mind-blowing music, that heart orchestration always on my fringes, absorbing hours of my life for complete seconds at a time. But a buzzing was pursuing me from my insides, floating in me, grabbing all the edges, demanding attention, saying names, bringing images, sorting all the parts of her anatomy, saying our angels were off sleeping someplace. She kissed me again. Oh, Maye, you may. Her breath licked at me; sweet fire, sweet taste of something new, then an awareness of newness, a saline edge, the spring marsh alive, brackish, reed grass like razor blades, horseshoe crabs with their spikes at Rumney Marsh, salt coming home from the sea, summer wind in the reeds all night long beside Baker Hill. I could have dived into the mouth of her body. It was hot and lovely and had a scent that tantalized me, one that I had never known. Not a Ginnie taste. Not an Ethel taste. Alive, it was, and after me the whole way! I was sure I was going to lose my breath, that my heart would stop. Would Ginnie ever be like this? Could she? Ethel?

Maye guided my hands again, as I was limp and afraid to move them. She put one of my hands on her back and the other one in front. I was frozen stiff. My heart was pounding. Oh, that patch at her back was thick and lustrous, yet as imaginably fine as some golden flax, as if it had been spun out of a fairy tale, some princess or a naughty Goldilocks thing come to rest with me, but dry and oh so soft and caressing my fingers. And rising on the air the whole world of newness. It came out of that everlasting dream world of fancy and daring and sat in the small of her back just above her buttocks. I was totally disoriented for a few seconds, wondering where I was, what side was up, if Harvey was lost here also. Then, driven by another motor, another propulsion on its own, mindless, madness perhaps or hunger, my other hand was suddenly inside her underpants, in that other patch, not as fine but slightly wiry and damp and liquid and the rich moistness beginning to run down my hand and its essence assailing me, a whole onslaught underway. She moved against my docile hand, again and again, and finally said the most magic words a boy could ever hear, "Take my underpants off, Tommy, take them off and throw them in the river."

The command was dark and without fear, without thought of refusal, and her voice was husky and absorbing and boggled my own thinking. I swore that if I could see, I would see some message in her eyes, as if it had been written just for me, yet was composed of words of my own making. My bell was ringing.

Some specific knowledge was looking for root at the back of my head. I felt it tingle in my fingers, move up my arms to further reception. It said I had crossed a wide barrier, that I was on the other side of forever. I was different. In a matter of these few minutes I was different, and I knew it. I would never be the same again. A new dynamic, at a new beachhead, had come into place. It was raw and eager, had a breath of its own, and would follow me everywhere from that very moment.

Maye continued, with her hands, with her words. "This is your night. I have watched you watching me. I liked it, all of it, you in the darkness and me in a kind of light, me being watched. Perhaps from the first I knew you were there, at an edge of darkness. And I know everything that's been said about me, every word down at the pool room, in the locker room at the field, at recess at school. But for now, do all the things I tell you. Just like I tell you. Oh, yes, just like that...make me beautiful again...just for one night...oh, yes, just for this night... beautiful all over...beautiful again...I am nothing but a dreamy child again... we are children again and I will dream of you tonight and tomorrow night, but we can never be together again. Oh, yes, like that. Oh, yes. You know it all now, don't you? And all that other stuff. He thinks he loves me. He's so unhappy, like I was unhappy. He's a tortured man who can cry the hours away, or let them get away from him. Oh, he is such a man when he doesn't cry. And he wants to show me off, but he can't. It will never happen, I know. I will be banished forever to this kind of darkness. I must have been born for it."

Mystery was rushing through her, making demands, gathering words and visions, as if owning her for the time being. "Throw my underpants out far enough so they will ride off in the current, so they'll go right down the river. Our night is here and they will be gone on the current. They will go to sea. Maybe they'll ride forever, and you can think of that for always, where the touch of your hand has gone, from here and out to sea, but we'll be done here tonight. Never come near me again. Go your way and I'll go mine. For the gift of this night, all I ask is just that. That you go on past this. He will, in time, go his way too."

She never once said his name. Maye never once said "Harvey," never once said what he was capable of, what he liked, what made a difference with him. In that way she was true blue.

I came out of this buzzing sound that had inhabited me and she was walking across the bridge. I heard her heels click for perhaps thirty steps and she was in the path heading across the field. The tossed, wet underpants were gone down river, I assumed. I dressed feverishly, lost one sock, threw the second one away onto the water, walked up the path. The peepers had come back from the whole length of the river, and the crickets from a hundred fields, and a slight zephyr of air brought her back to my senses so that I could taste her again. I thought of Ginnie and Ethel again. There was a difference, but it would narrow. Somehow, some way, it would narrow, and become.

We won our first three football games. I got into one of them late in the fourth quarter. Harvey's son Rex had exploded for five touchdown in the three games. I could spot Harvey and his pals in the stands. I kept thinking about him and Maye, wondering how that was going on.

In the middle of the next week, Harvey Upham fell down carrying his wife down the stairs. They said he died of a severe and massive heart attack. His wife was back to her bed. Their son's teammates all went to the wake and the funeral. Rex didn't play the following game. We lost by a touchdown. When he came back we won four more in a row, and lost the last game. Rex was an All-Star on all the local papers and was promised a scholarship at Boston College. The season was over and I was wandering again.

I came up from the Center well after eleven o'clock one night three weeks after Thanksgiving. The darkness was still there along Central Street. There were few lights about, and no moon. Earlier, on the way out to visit Ethel, I had seen a dozen men writing with pens on a variety of notepads, each man fully suited, some with felt hats, walking across every inch of the Iron Works site. People said plans were made, that the reconstruction was about to begin. History was being reworked.

I was almost up to the path that leads down to the river, when I heard the engine of Harvey Upham's big sedan. A single car door slammed shut in its usual coding, and the engine slipped into gear. I knew that Maye Tuong was being carried off again to wherever, this time by Harvey's son Rex, my teammate. I wondered if Rex had ever been brought along in the back seat on those other rides.

But Ethel made me think about something else, before I thought one last time about Chinatown and Shanghai and Maye Tuong riding around Saugus Center in a rickshaw and my end of the river squeezing itself onto another page of history.

The Man Who Hid Music

O ne day, at the little house where the dowser used to live, a kind-looking man with a beard came carrying all he owned on an A-frame on his back. He set the A-frame on the ground and looked at the small house needing much work. Muscles moved under his shirt.

"Whose house is this?" he said to some children playing at an edge of a field. This was the place where the mountain came to a rest, but the river had not been found as yet.

One of the boys said, "It used to belong to the dowser, but he went away." The boy used a stick to walk with, as one leg was slightly crooked and made him lean.

"Why did he go away?" the man said, looking closely at the stick the boy had to use.

"People laughed at him," answered the boy. When he looked at his friends some of them began to chuckle and grin. "Don't," the boy said. His sandy hair caught the wind; his eyes were hazel and steady.

"If I want to fix this house up and live here, tell me who I have to see." The children could see some of the tools hanging on the man's A-frame. On edges where the sun touched them the tools shone brightly as if they had been polished with gems.

"See Macklow the mayor. He lives down there where those walls meet." The boy pointed across the wide fields. "He'll be on his porch listening to the birds of the fields. My name is Max. What is your name?"

The man of the tools smiled at Max's description of the mayor. "My name does not count, only what I do," he said. He walked across the fields and soon had the house to work on. At first it was just the children who watched him fix doors and steps and windows, but soon other people, including Macklow, came to watch. All the time he used tools the man whistled different tunes. At his work he was a happy man.

The house was soon a sparkling and cozy place with no lopsided boards and no broken steps and no windows free to the air. When the man needed wood, he put the empty A-frame across his shoulders and walked off toward the mountain and the forests. In the evening he returned with a pile of wood of all lengths sitting across the back of his shoulders.

"Some day, perhaps soon," he said one day to the children watching him, and a few of the older people, "I will have a surprise for you." As usual, just at dusk, the man took some of his wood he had been working with and brought it inside the little house. The light went on inside so they knew he was still working.

Nobody knew what he was working on. But the light burned long into many nights.

And soon, to everyone's surprise, a garden was also blooming behind the house. Macklow was really surprised because his own fields were slow. Nobody had seen the kindly man walk out of his little house at night, time after time, and put buckets of water on his little garden. The dowser's well was right inside the little house and those who had laughed at the dowser never knew about the well and the sweet water it gave up.

One morning the man came out of his house and gave a new stick to Max. It was much better that Max's old stick, and was smooth and polished and very strong. Max was proud of his new stick and could walk faster with it. Over his head he waved it and showed it off to his friends.

On each morning from then on the man began to build a fence around the house and the garden. At first he put up strong posts, then mounted stringers between the posts. When all the posts and stringers were mounted and connected, he began to place upright pickets on the stringers.

Now and then one of the pickets would cause someone to laugh and titter about its strange shape. Some of the pickets were not as pretty and straight as others. Some indeed looked odd and out of place. But the man kept adding both straight and odd-looking pickets to the fence.

"See," Macklow said one day when village people were talking about the fence, "he brings out what he brought into the house the night before. What he does to it is a mystery, but let us not laugh at him. We laughed at the dowser and he went away in the night. This man is a kind man and has promised us a surprise. Do not laugh at him, no matter what his fence looks like." When he looked at little Max with the new stick, Max and Macklow swapped nods, as if they shared a secret.

But laughter, though, did come each day, at the way the fence looked, at crooked or bent pickets, at the weird shapes of some of them.

Then the day came when all the vegetables in the garden were ripe and the bizarre fence circled the house. The man seemed pleased and put his tools down except for one knife and walked off toward the forest. He came back with one small piece of wood. From that piece of wood he whittled a small whistle. When he blew into the whistle he found only one note, a pure note, but only one note.

There was more small laughter and chuckling, but Macklow, remembering the dowser, thinking about the new ripe garden and his own slow crops, would not laugh. Nor would Max with his new walking stick.

One morning the man spoke to some people looking at his crop and studying what he had done to fix the house and the fence he had placed all around it. "I have hidden the music here. Music is a part of the soul. Music is part of the water too. And water is part of the soul. Whoever finds the music I have hidden can have this house, for Macklow says it is mine to give."

Macklow nodded his head.

In the morning the man was gone. The tools were gone. The A-frame was gone.

People pored over the house trying to find the music. They did not know what they were looking for. But they found the dowser's well at the back end of the house and wondered at that. Macklow marveled at the well. However, he made sure none of them disturbed the things the man had done to fix the house.

It was curious. Nobody could find the music. None of them knew what they were looking for. But Max kept playing the whistle and kept hearing the note. He would sit on the porch and blow the whistle until people began to be bothered by it and asked him to stop.

But Max also knew that note deep inside his head.

For weeks people looked for the music. But they did not know what they were looking for.

And then, one morning as he walked past the house, Max hit one of the pickets with his stick.

Oh, how his heart pounded in his chest. How it grew it seemed that it might explode.

It was the same note from the whistle. The exact same, beautiful note.

Back to the gate he went, at the same note-sounding picket and began to walk around the house, his stick slapping against each picket in turn, the way boys have done ever since going by church and school yard fences.

And Macklow looked and the people looked and they all heard the music coming from the fence pickets as Max, walking without his stick support for the first time in his life, played elegant music on the ugly looking pickets with the stick the man had carved. The circled fence played out a whole lovely tune.

And Macklow saw to it that Max and his mother had themselves a new house to live in, at the place where the mountain comes to rest and the river is not yet found.

Leaving for Vivier

The boy slipped from a hole in the remnants of a stone wall that marked one section of his grandfather's farm, crawled behind a small tree, and stared down into the valley. At least a week before, shells from distant cannon and mortar had severed the wall in dozens of places, and a crater sat where the chicken house used to be. The pig pen, from the dead of winter, was a new abomination, with the small fence heaved asunder and unknown body parts strewn every which way.

The Alsace winter of 1944 had been cold and worn with misery, but now, as he breathed new air, he could see buds on the trees on the floor of the valley and across nearby hills. From a distance he heard a bird call for a friend, and heard the answer. It made him smile for the first time in the morning. Then, far off, he saw a group of soldiers marching back into their small encampment with three enemy soldiers walking ahead of them, docile prisoners at the points of rifles, their hands clasped atop their heads. All the soldiers, front and back, the catching and the caught, trudged tired and worn, as if they were weary of the war, too weary to carry on. Days earlier great tanks, support vehicles, and hundreds of soldiers had passed through the valley and gone ahead. The boy could see their tracks trenchant in the new grass trying for green, in the matted grain fields on early legs, and coming out of the small, now distorted copse of maples and birches at the edge of the hill that for a hundred years had provided heat for the family.

As he looked down on the small group, he didn't know who to feel sorry for, the ones up front or the ones with the rifles. More than a dozen of them were armed with rifles. The sun bounced off their helmets and parts of their weapons. The bird called again.

"Just let us know if any soldiers are coming this way," his grandfather had said as he ushered him out of the house that morning. "Give us enough time so we can hide a few things." The old man had patted him on the head, the way he did on most errands these days, the way his father had patted him, the way he had learned.

On some days the boy had forgotten what his father looked like. He'd been dead for more than two years, shot by one side or the other at a tumultuous point of the war. So the boy didn't know who he hated. But he hated somebody. Anybody who came on their land stood a good chance.

He saw an officer come out of a tent and stand at the head of the soldiers. Then all the soldiers of the small camp gathered around the officer, who was apparently talking to them. He saw the officer make gestures and point back toward Viviers. He could not hear the officer's voice and tried to read his body language. Soon many of the soldiers ran to places in the campsite. Some began to shave, some to wash their faces or strip to the waist and wash themselves. All of them had come to life in an instant, as if the war was over, but it was surely not. A whole fleet of planes, big ones, were flying overhead, the broad sky filled with aircraft as far as he could see, the noise another part of the everlasting whine even when he thought a small silence had been earned.

Three of the soldiers stood still where they were, not at attention it appeared, but the officer continued talking to them, making more gestures the boy could not understand. Then the three prisoners were put inside a fenced enclosure, and the three soldiers the officer had been talking to took up guard positions. Another low sound, a hum, came to him. At the end of the small valley the boy saw two big trucks coming down the narrow road. The trucks, big army trucks, stopped at the campsite. After a while all the soldiers, including the officer, climbed up on the trucks, but not the three on guard, or the three prisoners still inside the fence. The trucks turned around and headed back toward Viviers, down the narrow road, becoming dark dominoes moving.

The guards sat down. The prisoners sat down inside the enclosure. Each looked like they were talking to their own kind. A bird called, one answered and another. All six men looked back toward Viviers and then across the valley where the bird had called again, or one like it, or one near it. Buds, green as good vines, jittered nervously on tree limbs as a small spring breeze lifted its arms and waved. The boy smiled and said hello under his breath.

But the smile made the boy feel sad. For at that same moment he remembered his sister, and the day she walked into the barn just ahead of some soldiers coming from behind the barn. She had not seen them and at least three of them followed her inside. He was hidden where his grandfather had left him, in a hole against one wall, the hole he just now slipped out of as he watched more soldiers, the ones with the prisoners. His grandfather had told him never to leave the hole while he was away and told his sister to stay hidden in the barn, but he knew she just had to feed their last animal, a mere piglet. He remembered hearing her screaming and he cried again, as he had on many days since. The soldiers left the barn after a long while. When his sister did not come out of the barn, he crept out of the hole and went to look for her.

She was dead, hanging from a beam in the barn. She was fourteen. Her clothes had been torn from her and she had tied some in knots to cover herself. The boy knew everything in an instant. The soldiers did not tie the noose. They did not toss the rope over the beam in the barn. They did not get her to stand on the milk stool that still leaned against one wall. But they were the hangmen. He knew it. He knew his sister.

It was the same day he heard the distant whine, the whine as it drew closer. It was the whine and roar of war and all its collected parts coming one at a time, or in continuing odd pairs, the machinery of war, sounding out itself in pieces but slowly building its full way. At first it was as faint as if an old playmate, Rene or Jean, had called from the next farm or the next hill, coming as it did into a part of one ear, at the edge of all sound, at the edge of the belief of sound, and then came all the pieces of sound: the single bullets slicing in the air, the soft thump against wood or clatter on rock at the end of poor aim, the arc of shells screaming inside his head harsh as a close whistle, the distant impulses that sent the shells toward him and the farm and the tremors in the earth, the vibrations in the air as strong as evil itself, and soon the yelling rising up on its legs, the orders, the cries of terror and fright, the war itself, the terrible machine rolling across the land the way plows once wandered, turning everything over, the very land itself and all it offered up, the vines, the grass, the golden grains, day into night, night into day, silence into noise, noise into silence, peace into war. The awful impulses that came with war.

With his grandfather off on the strange errands he often attended to, the boy kept watch on the encampment. He knew that more than silence and language separated the two small groups of soldiers down below. He tried to imagine all their differences and was hounded by the difficulty the problem presented. Nothing, he believed, could be resolved from distance. More whines arose. More planes passed over the valley, like a cloud of sparrows erroneously leaping south. The sound roared in his ears as the war continued beyond him and the farm and his secret hole in the ground.

For more than an hour the three soldiers on guard were talking and obviously arguing. One of them kept pointing over his shoulder, back to where the trucks had gone. Gestures and wild motions came out of him as if he were on stage, in a wild drama. Perhaps it was a comedy. The boy did not know. Then the lead actor, the one with the motions and gestures, walked to the enclosure, opened the gate and pointed off to the other end of the valley, where the war was. The prisoners came out of the enclosure and began to walk off toward the war. Then they began running, stumbling, falling, rising, running again. The three guards put their rifles to shoulder and shot them in the back.

In the silence that followed the guard soldiers began to clean themselves. Two shaved, one washed his torso completely. All three were waving their arms in odd motions, marionettes against drab canvas. Finally all three of them, rifles over their shoulders, began to walk toward Viviers.

Now the boy knew who he hated.

About the Cover Artist

Jeff Fioravanti is an expressive realist painter, who offers to the viewer works of art that are not only representations of the subject, but images of mood and feeling that entice and stimulate the viewer to make an emotional and personal connection to each piece.

Jeff, a champion and friend to the preservation of America, is a technically sound and gifted artist, who has shown his talents in regional, national and international juried and invitation only exhibitions, resulting in many top honors and awards as a participant in these shows. Included in his awards/honors are: inclusion in "Who's Who in American Art"; "Who's Who in America"; the "Terry Ludwig Gold Award" at the 7th Annual Pastel Painter's of Maine national juried exhibition; the "Michael Allen Company Award: Best in Show" at the 7th annual "Renaissance in Pastel" national Juried exhibition, sponsored by the Connecticut Pastel Society; "First Runner-Up" at the Pastel Painters Society of Cape Cod's 5th annual national Juried exhibition; the "Olympian Corporation Award" at the "Pastels USA," national Juried exhibition, sponsored by the Pastel Society of the West Coast; "Best in Show, Pastels" at the ArtsAround Boston national Juried exhibition; and he was a finalist in past years' "Pastel 100," juried competition of top pastel artists from around the world, sponsored by *Pastel Journal Magazine*.

Jeff has judged exhibitions including the 8th annual, "Renaissance in Pastel," and has been featured in such publications as *American Artist Magazine* (November 2005), and *Pastel Artist International*, (May/June/July 2000) in their prestigious section: "Masters of Pastel Artists of the World, USA Showcase."

A member of several national pastel societies, with the added distinction/ honor of "Signature Artist Member" in the prestigious and world-renowned Pastel Society of America (New York, N.Y.), as well as The Connecticut Pastel Society (Meriden, CT.) and the Pastel Painters Society of Cape Cod (Barnstable, MA.). Fioravanti's works are currently held in many corporate and private collections throughout the US and Europe, as well as in the permanent collection of the Cape Ann Historical Museum.

Jeff resides in Lynn, Massachusetts, and is currently represented by and exhibiting at Art Research Associates gallery in South Hamilton, MA, and Art3 gallery in Manchester, NH.